MARVEL MULTIVERSE MISSIONS

MOON KNIGHT

AGE OF ANUBIS

JONATHAN GREEN

ACONYTE

FOR MARVEL PUBLISHING

VP Production & Special Projects: Jeff Youngquist
Editor, Special Projects: Sarah Singer
Manager, Licensed Publishing: Jeremy West
VP, Licensed Publishing: Sven Larsen
SVP Print, Sales & Marketing: David Gabriel
Editor in Chief: C B Cebulski

© 2023 MARVEL

First published by Aconyte Books in 2023
ISBN 978 1 83908 257 3
Ebook ISBN 978 1 83908 258 0

Cover art by Xteve Abanto • Interior art by Xteve Abanto • Book design by Nick Tyler
Technical assistance by Victor Cheng • Series development by Tim Dedopulos

Distributed in North America by Simon & Schuster Inc, New York, USA
Printed in the United States of America
9 8 7 6 5 4 3 2 1

ACONYTE BOOKS

An imprint of Asmodee Entertainment Ltd
Mercury House, Shipstones Business Centre
North Gate, Nottingham NG7 7FN, UK
aconytebooks.com // twitter.com/aconytebooks

"You heard that?" Moon Knight says, sounding even more surprised than you do. He turns fully toward you, clearly examining you in a new light. "You heard Khonshu speak?"

"Yes, but Khonshu is mistaken – I'm no high priest."

Your mind is awhirl; you have never encountered anything like this before. But then again, if mummies can come to life, then why wouldn't you be able to hear the voice of a god?

"Come with me!" Moon Knight commands, and you feel compelled to obey.

You haven't met the vigilante before – you haven't met any super heroes before, in person – but, considering your field of study, you have followed news of his exploits with interest. Meeting him this night feels almost… ordained.

MORE SUPER HERO ACTION

For Mattie, my own Marvel super fan.

WELL MET, TRAVELLER!

This is an adventure gamebook. If you don't know what that is, maybe flick on through the next few pages for a moment, then head back here…

Yep, that's right, lots of numbered entries. You start at entry **1** but must then decide which numbered entry to turn to next, according to what the text tells you. You do not just plough straight on to read the next page in order. Not because it's secret, but because it'll be really confusing, and that's no fun. We want you to have a good time.

In this adventure, you take on the role of an Egyptologist who assists Moon Knight as he fights to thwart the plans of both gods and monsters. In addition to making decisions to help unravel the mystery you are wrapped up in, you are going to need to keep track of some stuff and roll some six-sided dice. So grab paper and pencil, or open up a text file, and track down a six-sider or two.

You have three core statistics in this book: **MIGHT**, **MYSTIC**, and **MIND**, represented by numbers. *Might* relates to combat, *Mystic* has to do with persuasion, and *Mind* is a reflection of how well you are able to concentrate. Easy. They will change a lot over the course of your travels, and you'll use them often, so keep a close eye on them. If a stat goes negative, then it makes your rolls and chances of success worse, and in certain circumstances it might even be game over, so try to stay healthy. As a reward for reading this introduction before diving in, ignore what it tells you at entry **88**, **19**, or **260** (which one you hit will depend on your first choice) and instead, start with each of these statistics at 3. Well done, you.

There is also a whole range of secondary **QUALITIES** you might pick up… {ECLIPSED}, for example. Qualities are always in {CAPITALS IN CURLY BRACKETS}. Secondary qualities start afresh each new time you play, so if the book tells you to take a Quality you haven't encountered yet, that Quality starts with a score of 1. Keep track of them because they can seriously change how events unfold. If there's ever a reference to a bonus awarded by a Quality you don't currently have, you don't get that bonus – maybe try to find and acquire it.

You'll also find physical **OBJECTS** you can take with you, and they're always marked in [Square Brackets] to show they're special. They might provide bonuses or help with specific situations. Or not. You can have up to **five** objects at once. After that, to take something new, you must drop (cross off) something you already have. Some objects are used up when you employ them, so can be deleted at that point.

During your adventures, you're going to run into **tests**, **fights**, **minigames**, and **puzzles**. They're all clearly labeled. Just follow the instructions at the time. Oh, and there are also some entries with no obvious link leading to them. The clues on how to find them are in the text, mostly. They're worth your while to sniff out.

You can get killed, at least fictionally. Terminal mistakes finish with **The End.** If that happens, your adventure is over. Chalk it up to experience and try again from the start. There are several quite different routes through the book, so you definitely won't see everything in one playthrough anyway.

Lastly, as you progress, you'll be given ACHIEVEMENTS after certain groovy choices or results. There's a full list at the end of the book. When you're given an achievement, tick it off the list – these are good for multiple playthroughs. If you're reading this in ebook format, alas, you'll have to keep notes somewhere else.

There are also some SUPER-ACHIEVEMENTS listed at the end of the book for finishing the adventure with certain hard-to-find objects or qualities in your possession.

And that's all there is to it. Now it's time to begin your journey – turn the page!

1

It is eerily quiet in the new Egyptian Gallery on the top floor of the Metropolitan Museum of Art. Moonlight enters through the skylights high above, bathing the exhibits in its monochrome glow. The new display of ancient Egyptian artifacts opens to the public tomorrow, and this is your last chance to check that everything is just so before the great and the good of New York descend on the museum in the morning. It may have been your boss Dr Uraeus, the museum's new curator, who arranged for the exhibition to be put on here, but it was really you, as an experienced Egyptologist, who was tasked with making his dream a reality.

The centerpiece of the exhibition is the sarcophagus of King Akharis, a forgotten pharaoh of the Eighteenth Dynasty. It is a remarkable treasure, over eight feet tall, carved from cedar wood and covered in gold, decorated with thousands of hand painted hieroglyphs.

But what's this? What is the Book of the Dead doing in the cabinet next to the sarcophagus? You had placed it at the entrance to the exhibition. And why has the papyrus scroll been turned from the painting of Anubis weighing the soul of the pharaoh to the spell known as "The Opening of the Mouth?" And what is the canopic jar with a lid in the shape of a jackal's head doing in the cabinet to the right of Akharis's coffin? You had displayed it with the other three jars in a case at the back of the gallery.

Someone has rearranged the exhibits without asking your permission first!

The sound of footsteps on the marble floor has you turning to see Dr Uraeus entering the exhibition gallery. "Magnificent, isn't it?" he says. "The burial treasures of King Akharis, on display to the public for the first time."

"Er, yes," you agree, "but, doctor, can you tell me why the exhibits have been moved? This is not how I originally arranged them."

"I thought they made more of an impact like this," he replies, a self-satisfied smile on his face. "Don't you agree?"

You are about to answer that you definitely do not agree, when the sarcophagus suddenly starts to shake. Startled, you take a step back. A terrifying chill rushes over you. Something is hammering on the inside of the coffin lid, as if trying to get out!

What could possibly be inside? Overcoming your fear, you move to help Dr Uraeus open the sarcophagus. In that instant, the ancient wood splinters as a bandaged hand punches straight through it. The hand is withdrawn again and at the next punch the lid comes clean off, and crashes to the floor.

What emerges is a giant of a man, seven feet tall and bound from head to toe in ancient, stained bandages. Where the bandages have loosened over time, you see withered, blistered flesh. The wrappings that cover his face part as the Mummy opens his mouth. A rasping howl, that makes you think of a sandstorm howling over the desert, issues forth, while the yellow orbs of eyes that first looked upon the world thousands of years ago, burn with rage and madness. Take **+1 {HAPPY HALLOWEEN}**.

The Mummy's physique is truly monstrous. Dr Uraeus gives a strangled cry, turns tail, and flees from the gallery, as the bandaged giant reaches for you with hands hooked into clutching claws.

Your heart thuds in your chest. What do you want to do?

To turn tail and run after Dr Uraeus, turn to **62**.

To look for a suitable weapon with which to defend yourself, turn to **101**.

To look for something else to use against the Mummy, turn to **21**.

2

Uh oh, it looks like you've taken a wrong turn. If you're reading this because you finished the first section and just kept on going, we must warn you that you are going to get confused, and probably bored, very quickly. This book really only makes sense if you hop from entry to entry, according to the choices you make and the directions you're given. We suggest you go back and decide how you're going to deal with the Living Mummy.

Then again, maybe you're here because you think this section is the solution to one of the puzzles in the book. Sorry, wrong again. Whoever said that finding all those Easter Eggs was going to be easy? But award yourself an Achievement anyway. ACHIEVEMENT: *Could Do Better*.

But perhaps you're here because you are actively looking for Achievements. OK then, fair enough, here's one on us. ACHIEVEMENT: *Trophy Hunter*.

Now go back to whatever it was you were doing before, which might mean going back to **1**.

3

"Naturally," Mr Knight replies.

Returning to the limousine, he accesses a computer terminal inside the car, pulling up a map of the surrounding city streets. Speaking into a communicator on his wrist, he launches several small drones from a sunroof hatch in the top of the car and then instructs them to scan the area of Fifth Avenue, from 54th to 52nd Street for explosives.

Within no time at all, the electronic voice of the limousine's "driver" says, *"One explosive device located. Relaying coordinates now."*

Mr Knight consults the data before exiting the vehicle a second time. Take **+1 {KNIGHTED}** and **+1 MIND**.

"It's Knowles," he says. "He's carrying the bomb himself."

Crossing the police cordon, he strides purposefully down Fifth Avenue. When a number of officers go to stop him, Detective Flint waves them back. You join the disheveled detective at the barricade the police have set up across the entire width of the road and watch, wondering what will happen next.

You realize that there is someone approaching from the other end of Fifth Avenue. He is dressed in a manner that reminds you of a medieval knight, but one who has joined a biker gang and rides a motorcycle rather than a warhorse. He appears to be holding a trigger, or maybe the device itself, in his right hand. But will he dare to activate it or will he back down in the face of Mr Knight's apparent fearlessness? Only a few yards stand between them now.

Make an intimidation test. Roll one die and add your **MIGHT** and **MYSTIC** to it. What's the result?

Total of 9 or more: turn to **116**.

8 or less: turn to **156**.

Moon Knight is so focused on making it through the underworld as quickly as he can that he fails to notice the stirring in the gray-brown effluent stream beside the walkway. This means that you are both taken by surprise when something monstrous bursts from the current, propelling itself bodily out of the water to land on the grilled path in front of you. Take **-1 MIND**.

The thing must be over seven feet tall, as it crouched to avoid hitting its head against the curved brick roof of the tunnel. You can see it quite clearly, bathed as it is in the jaundiced light of the caged lamps. It is humanoid in form and covered in a thick green reptilian hide. Its face is almost fish-like, with an ugly mouth full of needle-sharp teeth, and you assume that the two fin-like projections on either side of its head are its ears. Another spiny ridge runs the length of its back, and you can tell that its hands and feet are webbed.

The creature fixes you with burning red eyes and a sibilant hiss escapes its fishy lips. Take **+1 {HAPPY HALLOWEEN}**.

Make an aggression test. Roll one die and if it is equal to or lower than your **{UNLOCKED}**, if you have any, turn immediately to **33**.

If the result is higher, what do you think Moon Knight should do?

Attack the amphibious horror: turn to **33**.

Try and talk to it: turn to **53**.

5

The cop's eyes alight on the golden, sickle-shaped sword resting on your lap. His eyes go wide, and he goes for his gun.

At that moment you hear Khonshu inside your head once more. In a voice that is as smooth as milk and as rich as honey you hear him say, *You could take up that weapon and cut the fool down where he stands.*

"There's no need for that," Mr Knight says with a weary sigh as you offer him an apologetic shrug. You're not sure if he is addressing the cop or Khonshu.

"Put the weapon on the floor and step out of the vehicle!" the police officer shouts, pointing the gun at you.

Mr Knight takes a deep breath as he adjusts the cuffs of his white Egyptian cotton shirt. You tense, not knowing what he might do next...

If you think Mr Knight will reason with the cop calmly and logically, turn to **238**.

If you think he will use his powers of persuasion on the cop, turn to **293**.

If you think he will use the brief but sudden application of force, turn to **263**.

6

Moon Knight takes Kraven the Hunter's [Whip] from you and lassos the lever with it, pulling it down. This immediately shuts off the flow of sand entering the chamber, but that is not all it does. With a grinding of stone, the block that dropped down sealing the doorway begins to rise.

Moon Knight ties off the other end of the whip around the plinth, so that the stone can't drop down again, and as soon as the space beneath it is large enough for him to pass under he makes his escape, calling for you to follow him.

Remove the [Whip] from your Inventory and take the ACHIEVEMENT: *Necessity is the Mother of Invention*.

Now turn to **98**.

7

"But I can do more than just that for you," Doctor Strange goes on.

"Will you come with us?" you ask, excitedly.

"No, I must remain here and ensure the esoteric wards that protect the Sanctum Sanctorum remain in place. For there are dark forces that would use such a distraction as a zombie invasion in an attempt to breach its walls and plunder its secrets. But I can help to prepare you for what you might face when you finally catch up with N'Kantu. Come with me."

The Sorcerer Supreme leads you through his mystical stronghold to what is quite clearly a library, although some of the books have been chained to the sturdy shelves, and rattle as you enter, as if trying to free themselves, while half-unrolled scrolls cover almost every available surface, including the green leather of a reading desk.

"There is nothing more powerful than knowledge," Doctor Strange says as he takes a dusty papyrus from a shelf and starts to unroll it over the top of the other scrolls, "and I am more knowledgeable than most. Is there anything you have come across, any ancient artifacts perhaps, that you would like to know more about?"

If you have a **[Khopesh]** and want to ask about that, turn to **71**.

If you have an **[Ankh]** and want to ask about that, turn to **93**.

If you just want to find out more about the canopic jar N'Kantu stole, turn to **113**.

8

"I am Khonshu's vengeance made flesh," Mr Knight says, the enmity dripping from his words, "and there is much I have to avenge when it comes to Carson Knowles."

With that, ignoring the police cordon, Mr Knight sets off down Fifth Avenue on foot. When several officers go to stop him, Detective Flint stands them down. You join the disheveled detective at the barricade the police have set up across the entire width of the road and watch, wondering what Mr Knight intends to do. Take **+1 {UNLOCKED}**.

You realize that there is someone approaching from the other end of Fifth Avenue. He is dressed in a manner that reminds you of a medieval knight, but one who has joined a biker gang and rides a motorcycle rather than a warhorse. He is armed with a sword and a morning star. As you watch, Mr Knight chooses his own weapons, but what does he pull out from inside his jacket?

Baton: turn to **258**.

Crescent darts: turn to **275**.

Silver cesti: turn to **240**.

9

"What do you mean?" the other asks, his interest clearly piqued.

"N'Kantu the Living Mummy, and agent of Anubis, is loose in the city again. And he has the canopic jar of King Akharis."

"That doesn't sound good," Shadow Knight replies. But then his mood changes and he stiffens. "You wouldn't be making this up, would you, just to get yourself out of trouble?"

Moon Knight proceeds to do his best to persuade his brother that he is telling the truth. Obviously, there is a great sense of mistrust between the two of them. Take **+1 {GRANTED}**.

Make a persuasion test. Roll one die and add your **MYSTIC** and **MIND** to it. What's the result?

Total of 10 or more: turn to **232**.

9 or less: turn to **40**.

10

N'Kantu might have fled, but the zombified residents of New York remain and continue to attack any who aren't yet like them. Here, you see a homeless man with the pupilless stare and snapping teeth of one of the turned attack a traffic cop who has suddenly found himself on the wrong shift. There, a young woman plants her mouth on her bespectacled date but not in the way he might have hoped.

Whatever ritual the Living Mummy enacted, its effects have not been reversed by him leaving the scene of the crime.

"Where can he have gone?" you ask in despair.

"I could hazard a guess," Moon Knight says, "but we do not have the means to follow him, and right now we have more pressing concerns."

The zombies are pressing in from all sides and the horde is still growing at an exponential rate, as more and more succumb and join the undead throng crowding Times Square.

"We're either going to have to fight our way out or attempt to make a break for it while we still can." Moon Knight's hands turn into fists as he looks to you for guidance.

Which option do you favor: fight or flight? Or do you have another idea?

If you want to fight the zombies, turn to **107**.

If you want to flee, turn to **211**.

11

You pass the [Orb of Belgaroth] over his body. Before your eyes, you see tiny cracks appear in the crystal ball. These rapidly multiply as the fabric of the sphere starts to disintegrate, returning to the silica sand from which it was originally formed. There is nothing you can do to stop the process as the sand trickles away between your fingers until the Orb is entirely gone. Take **+1 {FEARFUL}**.

Strike the **[Orb of Belgaroth]** from your Inventory, then turn to **31**.

12

As the wards glide and whirl across the invisible magical shield, they might change orientation, but you can see that there are only actually twelve different sigils in total.

Under your guidance, Moon Knight touches each one in turn. As his fingers make contact with the twelfth, you hear a pop, feel a burst of static charge in the air, and smell the distinct coppery aroma of ozone.

ACHIEVEMENT: *Genius Level Intellect.*

Now turn to **234**.

13

Bringing all his god-given power to bear, Moon Knight sprints up the remaining steps and, ignoring the winds of magic that batter him, lashes out at the Living Mummy. In response, N'Kantu places the jar on the floor so that his hands are free to throttle the chosen of Khonshu.

This is a boss fight!

Round one: roll two dice and add your **MIGHT** and, if you have any, your {**UNLOCKED**}, but deduct any {**AWED**} you may have. If the total is 14 or more, you win the first round.

Round two: roll two dice and add your **MIGHT** and, if you have any, your {**GRANTED**}. If you won round one, add 1. If the total is 15 or more, you win the second round.

Round three: roll two dice and add your **MIGHT** and, if you have any, your {**ECLIPSED**}. If you won round two, add 2. If the total is 16 or more, you win the third round.

Subtract 1 from the number of rounds you won and adjust your **MIGHT** by that much: this could range from **+2** if you won all three, to **-1** if you lost all three.

If you won at least two rounds, turn to **110**.

If you lost at least two rounds, turn to **125**.

14

Moon Knight hurls the device he recovered from Black Spectre at the lycanthrope. The grenade lands at the creature's feet and the wolfman fixes his burning red gaze on the matte black casing, like a dog following a stick that had been thrown for it.

Take **+1** {**WHO LET THE DOGS OUT?**} and the ACHIEVEMENT: *Fetch!*

The device detonates a split second later, filling the alleyway with a momentary miniature sun, then clouds of smoke, and a boom that leaves your ears ringing.

As the smoke clears you see that the Werewolf has fled.

Strike the [Tactical Grenade] from your Inventory, then turn to 280.

15

You brandish the artifact before the Grey Gargoyle, but whatever its powers may be, they do not appear to have any effect on the super villain. He snatches it from your hands, crushing it within his stony grasp, and casts it aside as if it were not some priceless ancient Egyptian treasure.

Take -1 MYSTIC and strike the [Ankh] from your Inventory, then turn to 241.

16

Opening his door, Mr Knight steps out of the limousine and calls to the nearest traffic cop he can see. "What appears to be the problem, officer?"

"Road's closed, sir," the cop says, confusion creasing his brow as he realizes he is talking to a smartly dressed man wearing a white mask. Bending down he peers inside the limo and gives you the once-over too.

If you are carrying a [Khopesh], turn to 5.

If not, turn to 34.

17

"The tenth plague," whispers Moon Knight in a tone of reverent awe and wonder. "N'Kantu is truly drawing on the malign power of the Darkhold."

"Was that not the death of the firstborn?" you say, feeling the cold hand of fear tie your guts in a knot.

"Yes… so why wasn't I affected?" he muses, as if thinking aloud. "I can only imagine it is because I am under the protection of Khonshu and, by extension, so are you."

Take +1 {ABRACADABRA}.

Now turn to **39**.

18

"Look out!" Moon Knight suddenly shouts, his warning echoing loudly within the confines of the sewer.

As you stumble to a halt, almost colliding with your companion, something monstrous bursts from the channel, propelling itself bodily out of the water to land on the walkway in front of you.

The thing must be over seven feet tall and is forced to crouch within the tunnel so it doesn't scrape its head against the curved brick roof. You can see it quite clearly, bathed as it is in the jaundiced light of the caged lamps. It is humanoid in form and covered in a thick green reptilian hide. Its face is almost fish-like, with an ugly mouth full of needle-sharp teeth, and you assume that the two fin-like projections on either side of its head are its ears. Another spiny ridge runs the length of its back, and you can tell that its hands and feet are webbed.

The creature fixes you with burning red eyes and a sibilant hiss escapes its fishy lips. Take +1 {HAPPY HALLOWEEN}.

What would you do if you were in Moon Knight's shoes?

Attack the amphibious horror: turn to **33**.

Try and talk to it: turn to **53**.

19

Before we continue with the adventure, let's set up the powers for your team of Moon Knight and the Egyptologist. There are three core stats: **MIGHT**, **MYSTIC**, and **MIND**. You remember that from the introduction, which you absolutely read, yeah? Hm.

Might represents Moon Knight's current strength, agility, and resilience. Very helpful for punching things, which will turn out to be useful any moment now, as well as throwing things, leaping over things, breaking things, and all sorts of other tasks you'll encounter in due course.

Mystic is a measure of how persuasive other people consider Moon Knight to be at the time, but it also has a supernatural element to it. It can be affected by events that might impact other people's perceptions, and by acts of god. Any god.

Mind indicates your team's current level of mental ability. It's handy for solving problems, spotting objects that are out of the way or hard to notice, and thinking up clever solutions on the fly. However, you will still have to solve the puzzles in this book on your own.

Your core stats will change repeatedly over the course of your adventure, so you'll need to keep track of them on a piece of paper or a digital equivalent. You start with **MIGHT** of 3, **MYSTIC** of 2, and **MIND** of 2.

Right – back to the action…

As the vigilante is checking on you, the Living Mummy grabs him from behind.

Make a martial arts test. Roll one die and add both your **MIGHT** and **MIND** to it. What's the result?

Total of 8 or more: turn to **281**.

7 or less: turn to **233**.

20

The lightning strikes the vigilante and sends him crashing to the ground. Take **-2 MIGHT**.

"How dare you attack me!" Dr Uraeus roars, a sibilant hiss behind his words.

Make a threat test. Roll two dice and add your **MYSTIC**, as well as any **{DARK POWER}** you might have. If you have a **[Khopesh]** in your Inventory, deduct 1, but if you have an **[Ankh]**, deduct 2 instead, or if you have an **[Eye of Horus]**, deduct 3. What is the final total?

20 or more: turn to **22**.

19 or less: turn to **37**.

21

You look around, your panicked gaze alighting on the glass display cabinet to the right of the sarcophagus. It contains three objects of interest.

First is the dusty looking canopic jar – a clay pot etched with hieroglyphs and sealed by a lid sculpted to look like the stylized head of a jackal. Second is a large golden ankh, a physical representation of the ancient Egyptian symbol known as the Key of Life. Third is an innocuous wooden staff.

Opening the cabinet, you grab one of the artifacts from inside, but which one?

If you take the **[Ankh]**, turn to **43**.

If you take the **[Canopic Jar]**, turn to **74**.

If you take the **[Staff]**, turn to **217**.

An unintelligible roar of rage draws your attention to N'Kantu, the agent of Anubis. He throws himself at Moon Knight, clearly determined to stop Khonshu's avatar from thwarting the plans of his master.

This is going to be a tough fight!

Round one: roll two dice and add your **MIGHT**, along with your {UNLOCKED}. If the total is 20 or more, you win the first round.

Round two: roll two dice and add your **MIGHT**, along with your {UNLOCKED}. If you won round one, add 1. If the total is 21 or more, you win the second round.

Round three: roll two dice and add your **MIGHT**, along with your {UNLOCKED}. If you won round two, add 2. If the total is 22 or more, you win the third round.

Subtract 1 from the number of rounds you won and adjust your **MIGHT** by that much: this could range from **+2** if you won all three, to **-1** if you lost all three.

> If you won round three, you have defeated the Living Mummy, but you are not out of danger yet: turn to **37**.
>
> If you lost round three, turn to **225**.

23

"There is dark magic at work," whimpers the Werewolf. "I sense the power of the Darkhold behind whatever is happening here."

"The Darkhold?" you ask.

"A book of evil spells," Moon Knight explains.

"And the source of my curse," adds Jack.

Take +1 {ABRACADABRA}.

There is evil afoot here," the Werewolf continues, "and we must sniff it out before its malign influence can spread too far."

Turn to **162**.

24

You already have your quarry and can't let yourself become distracted by the presence of other costumed characters.

But as Moon Knight steers the craft south, in the direction of Times Square, the figure on the roof rests what looks like a wide metal tube on his shoulder, and you see a puff of smoke as something is fired from the end.

You can't avoid telling Moon Knight now. "Look out!" you cry in alarm as the rocket streaks toward you through the cold night air.

Make an evasive maneuvers test. Roll two dice, add your **MIGHT** and **MIND**.

On a 12 or more: turn to **139**.

11 or less: turn to **56**.

25

There are zombies arriving from all directions now. The plague is spreading at an exponential rate, as more and more people become infected by the sickness that the Living Mummy's dark magic has unleashed upon the city.

The only sensible thing to do is flee as best you can.

Start at the street junction marked **START**. At each junction, roll one die to determine which way you go next. However, if you land at a junction where there are zombies, roll one die and if the result is 5 or 6, take **-1 MIGHT**.

When you reach the junction marked **END**, turn to **267**.

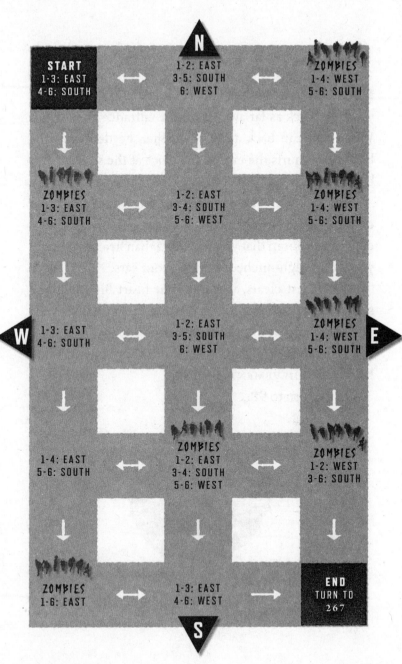

N

START
1-3: EAST
4-6: SOUTH

1-2: EAST
3-5: SOUTH
6: WEST

ZOMBIES
1-4: WEST
5-6: SOUTH

ZOMBIES
1-3: EAST
4-6: SOUTH

1-2: EAST
3-4: SOUTH
5-6: WEST

ZOMBIES
1-4: WEST
5-6: SOUTH

W

1-3: EAST
4-6: SOUTH

1-2: EAST
3-5: SOUTH
6: WEST

ZOMBIES
1-4: WEST
5-6: SOUTH

E

1-4: EAST
5-6: SOUTH

ZOMBIES
1-2: EAST
3-4: SOUTH
5-6: WEST

ZOMBIES
1-2: WEST
3-6: SOUTH

ZOMBIES
1-6: EAST

1-3: EAST
4-6: WEST

END
TURN TO
267

S

26

Moon Knight takes the [Tactical Grenade] from you, and you both back as far away from the entrance as possible. When you can back away no further, he depresses the button and hurls the explosive device at the stone that is blocking your way out of the treasure chamber.

For a moment, you can hear nothing but the susurrus of the sand pouring into the shrine. Then there is a concussive boom that you feel more than hear, that leaves you with a high-pitched whine in your ears.

As the dust clears, you feel your heart lift when you see that it has worked. The stone lies broken into several pieces and the way out is clear once more.

Strike the [Tactical Grenade] from your Inventory and take the ACHIEVEMENT: *Big Bang*.

Now turn to **98**.

27

As soon as you step through the portal the heat hits you, and you are forced to shield your eyes against the harsh daylight. On the other side of the doorway across reality it is an hour after midnight, but on this side the sun is already climbing over the endless desert that lies before you and behind you – in fact, everywhere you look.

"Hurry! The world depends on you!" are Doctor Strange's parting words, before the portal fizzles away to nothing.

"Egypt!" you declare, excited to return to a place you have visited many times during your career as an Egyptologist.

"Where else?" says Moon Knight.

You look around you, taking in every point of the compass. You can see nothing but sand in every direction. This place is so entirely lacking in water that even the air feels hot in your lungs.

A familiar booming voice suddenly echoes within your skull, making you cry out in alarm. *Seek out the temple Akharis built to honor his dark master!*

Judging from Moon Knight's startled reaction, he heard the voice too.

"I take it this isn't actually the location of the temple Akharis instructed to be built," you say, as the echo fades.

"No," Moon Knight confirms, "I suspect it will be somewhere in the mountains."

"In which case, how are we going to get there? I doubt I could make it much further than the horizon before the heat and thirst break me," you point out.

"Don't worry," Moon Knight says, and you can detect a wry tone in his voice. "I know a guy." With that, he speaks into the communicator attached to his wrist. "Spector calling Jean-Paul Duchamp. Moon Knight calling Jean-Paul Duchamp. C'mon Frenchie, pick up. It's Marc."

Accompanied by the crackle of static, a thickly accented voice comes back over the radio transmitter.

"Marc Spector? *Mon ami*, it is good to hear from you again. Are you in Egypt?"

"I am."

"Thank God for that. We need your help! *Mon dieu*, but this place is going mad." This Frenchie's agitation is evident, even over the crackling airwaves. "There are zombies everywhere, and their numbers are growing all the time as more and more people succumb to the plague they carry."

"That's why I'm here," says your companion. "But first I need your help. Can you pick us up?"

"Us? But of course, once I can clear a path through these unfortunate dead souls. Send me your coordinates."

Turn to **279**.

28

You hold the [Ankh] out before you and the effect is instantaneous. The beast man stops snarling as it becomes transfixed by the artifact. You can see the golden [Ankh] reflected in the Werewolf's blazing stare.

The next sound it makes, however, takes you utterly by surprise.

"Thank you," says the Werewolf.

Turn to **59**.

29

Being punched by the Grey Gargoyle is like being clubbed with a sack of cement, which is why Moon Knight uses his many martial arts skills to avoid letting any of the villain's punches land. Instead, he turns the villain's strength and weight against him, and in no time at all, the Grey Gargoyle is lying on the ground in a groaning heap.

"No one can defeat the Grey Gargoyle? Then are you *not* the fabulous Grey Gargoyle?" Moon Knight taunts his opponent. "You are not worthy to face the avatar of Khonshu in battle. I am his vengeance, and protector of those who travel by night. Now you have paid the price for threatening one of my own." Take **+1 MIGHT**.

Turn to **79**.

30

The Werewolf throws back his head and gives a long howl of triumph, while Moon Knight lies on the ground, steam rising from the dozens of wounds he has sustained at the claws of the savage beast.

Take **-1 MIGHT** and **-1 {ECLIPSED}**.

Clouds pass from before the face of the moon, and the alleyway is abruptly bathed in its chill light.

The Werewolf takes off, without even a glance back, while Moon Knight seems to be revitalized by the moonbeams.

"Come on," he says, getting to his feet once more, "we have to finish this."

Turn to **280**.

31

With the grinding of vast stone blocks rubbing against each other, the god-statue steps down from its plinth and reaches for you with a colossal stone hand.

Your mind is awhirl. You can't believe this is happening! What unearthly power is manifesting through the colossus? It's like you're in some kind of nightmare. Take **+1 {FEARFUL}**.

How do you want to respond to the stone giant's attack?

If you have a **[Khopesh]**, and want to use it now, turn to **66**.

If you have an [Ankh], and want to use it now, turn to **85**.

If you have a [Tactical Grenade], and want to use it now, turn to **111**.

If you have a [Vial of Serum], and want to use it now, turn to **269**.

If you have a [Crossbow], and want to use it now, turn to **278**.

If you have an [Alien Device], and want to use it now, turn to **287**.

If you want to run for it, turn to **52**.

32

Now nothing stands between Moon Knight and the Living Mummy!

You can feel the esoteric energies whirling about you, in a vortex of malign power, as more and more souls are drawn into the open canopic jar, meaning that more and more zombies are being created all the time. Take +1 {ABRACADABRA}.

Which of the following qualities has the highest score at present?

{UNLOCKED}: turn to **13**.

{GRANTED}: turn to **138**.

{ECLIPSED}: turn to **180**.

{KNIGHTED}: turn to **223**.

If they are all equal, turn to **209**.

33

The creature might look like something from out of a low budget, 1950s B-movie, but the Manphibian is actually an alien from a distant world and over a thousand years old. He pursued the being that killed his mate across several star systems in order to exact his revenge, his chase finally ending on Earth.

None of that fazes Moon Knight, who launches himself at the alien, bringing all his martial arts training and Khonshu-consecrated weapons to bear. Take +1 {UNLOCKED}.

This is a boss fight!

Round one: roll two dice and add your **MIGHT** and your {UNLOCKED}. If the total is 15 or more, you win the first round.

Round two: roll two dice and add your **MIGHT** and, if you have any, your {ECLIPSED}. If the total is 16 or more, you win the second round.

Round three: roll two dice and add your **MIGHT**, as well as your {UNLOCKED} and your {ECLIPSED}, if you have any. If the total is 17 or more, you win the third round.

Subtract 1 from the number of rounds you won and adjust your **MIGHT** by that much: this could range from **+2** if you won all three, to **-1** if you lost all three.

If you won two or more rounds, turn to **83**.

If you lost two or more rounds, turn to **99**.

34

"Is that Detective Flint over there?" Mr Knight asks, striding toward the roadblock without waiting for an answer.

"Sir, please return to your vehicle," the cop says, suddenly flustered by your companion's cast iron confidence, but Mr Knight ignores him. Thinking it's probably best if you stick together, you get out of the car and follow, as the young officer pleads with Mr Knight to return to his vehicle.

By the time you catch up with him, he is already in conversation with a downbeat-looking man in a trench coat.

"… right the way down to 52nd Street," you hear the detective saying as you join them, his bushy moustache wriggling like a caterpillar as he speaks. "He says he'll trigger the bomb if anyone goes anywhere near him."

"What does he want, Flint?" asks Mr Knight.

"I'll give you one guess."

"Me," Mr Knight says, his voice cold.

"Yeah. I was about to give you a call," adds Detective Flint.

Eager to be brought up to speed with what's going on, you make an interjection of your own. But what's it to be?

"Who's got a bomb?" Turn to **95**.

"Sounds like you and the bomber have history. Is there bad blood between the two of you?" Turn to **55**.

"Sounds like a job for Moon Knight." Turn to **75**.

"What about N'Kantu?" Turn to **154**.

35

As the Grey Gargoyle tries to touch you with his stone hands, you parry his attempts with the glittering, sickle-shaped sword. But the super villain's relentless advance forces you to back up against Moon Knight's limousine. With nowhere else to go, it can only be a matter of time before you become one of the Grey Gargoyle's statue victims.

Turn to **241**.

36

One second, you think you're looking at a skeletal bird, the next a cloud passes in front of the face of the moon and the statue ceases to glow, the voice becoming nothing more than an echo in your mind.

"High priest?" you gasp, finding your own voice again. "I'm not a high priest, I'm just a humble Egyptologist."

"You *heard* that?" Moon Knight says, sounding even more surprised than you do. He turns fully toward you, clearly examining you in a new light. "You heard Khonshu speak?"

"Yes, but Khonshu is mistaken – I'm no high priest."

Your mind is awhirl; you have never encountered anything like this before. But then again, if mummies can come to life, then why wouldn't you be able to hear the voice of a god?

"Come with me!" Moon Knight commands, and you feel compelled to obey.

You haven't met the vigilante before – you haven't met any super heroes before, in person – but, considering your field of study, you have followed news of his exploits with interest. Meeting him this night feels almost… ordained.

Turn to **236**.

37

Sudden vicious barking alerts you to the presence of Anubis's pets once more. The monstrous jackals throw themselves into the fray, but Moon Knight unthinkingly throws himself into their path, ready to teach them a lesson.

Moon Knight will have to deal with the jackals quickly.

Round one: roll two dice and add your **MIGHT**, along with your {UNLOCKED}. If the total is 14 or more, you win the first round.

Round two: roll two dice and add your **MIGHT**, along with your {UNLOCKED}. If the total is 15 or more, you win the second round.

If you won the second round, turn to **148**.

If you lost the second round, turn to **214**.

38

Moon Knight takes the [Sticks of Dynamite] and places them at the foot of the stone blocking the entrance. Binding their fuses together, he takes an ignition source from a utility pouch to light them, before the two of you try to shelter as best as you can, hunkering down behind the plinth on which the [Eye of Horus] rested.

For a moment you can hear nothing but the susurration of sand pouring into the chamber and the spitting of the fuse. The explosion, when it comes, is a concussive boom that you feel more than hear and leaves a piercing ringing in your ears.

As the dust clears, you feel your heart lift when you see that it has worked. The stone lies broken into several pieces and the way out is clear once more.

Strike the [Sticks of Dynamite] from your Inventory and take the ACHIEVEMENT: *Big Bang*.

Now turn to **98**.

39

You stare in horror as the people who just collapsed get back to their feet. But now they move with a strange jerkiness and leave any possessions they had been carrying where they dropped them. It would appear that they are more interested in the other people who are watching in disbelief at what is unfolding, just as you are. Take **+1 {AWED}**.

Anubis's lapdog must be brought to heel! comes the voice of Khonshu inside your head. You and Moon Knight look at each other. He heard the deity too, you are sure of it.

Someone screams and you see a middle-aged Latina lady topples to the ground as a young man wearing a backpack leaps on her and sinks his teeth into her shoulder. Just as quickly as he attacked her, he abandons her prone form, in search of another victim. But you barely have time to take another breath before the woman clambers to her feet again only to fall upon a startled Japanese tourist, snapping at his throat with slavering jaws. The same thing is happening all across Times Square.

You've seen enough late night double features to know what's going on. The population of NYC are turning into zombies! And you are right in the thick of things.

"It's not too late to stop this!" Moon Knight cries, throwing himself into the fray, and leaving you with no sensible choice but to follow.

ACHIEVEMENT: *Late Night Double Feature.*

Now turn to **299**.

40

Shadow Knight stiffens. "I don't believe you, brother. This is just another one of your lies. You're mad if you think I'm going to fall for it."

"You are in no position to question anyone's sanity," your companion rails.

"Oh, have I upset Khonshu's pet lunatic?"

"Well, you know what they say–"

Before Moon Knight can finish his sentence, his dark doppelganger attacks.

This is a brutal fight!

Round one: roll two dice and add your **MIGHT**. If the total is 16 or more, you win the first round.

Round two: roll two dice and add your **MIGHT**. If you won the first round, add 1. If your total is 15 or more, you win the second round.

If you won the second round, turn to **84**.

If you lost the second round, turn to **176**.

41

"Stained Glass Scarlet!" Moon Knight shouts, clearly recognizing your attacker as he leaps forward to engage the woman in battle. "You have attacked those who travel by night, so you must suffer the vengeance of Khonshu!"

In response, the woman merely gives an unintelligible snarl and raises her crossbow again. You are taken aback when you realize that she has already succumbed to the plague N'Kantu has unleashed upon the city. And she is not alone. More zombies are emerging from side-streets and alleyways and closing on your position.

This is a boss fight.

Round one: roll two dice and add your **MIGHT** and, if you have any, your {UNLOCKED}. If the total is 15 or more, you win the first round.

Round two: roll two dice and add your **MIGHT** and, if you have any, your {UNLOCKED} and your {ECLIPSED}. If the total is 16 or more, you win the second round.

Round three: roll two dice and add your **MIGHT** and, if you have any, your {UNLOCKED} and your {ECLIPSED}. If the total is 17 or more, you win the third round.

Subtract 1 from the number of rounds you won and adjust your **MIGHT** by that much: this could range from +**2** if you won all three, to -**1** if you lost all three.

If you won two or more rounds, your primary adversary drops her [Crossbow]: turn to **25**.

If you lost round three, Stained Glass Scarlet and the other zombies eventually manage to overwhelm Moon Knight by sheer force of numbers: turn to **107**.

42

"Good idea," says your companion. "We'll cover more ground faster that way, while keeping an eye out for N'Kantu at the same time."

He takes a baton from somewhere about his person and is about to deploy a grappling hook from the end when you point out that you will struggle to follow him if he favors that particular form of transportation.

He nods then, speaking into a communicator on his wrist, says, "Drone: to my position."

You do not have to wait long to see what he has summoned. It swoops down out of the night sky, as if a silvery sliver has detached itself from the moon and come to your aid. The sizable, crescent-shaped craft touches down and you barely know what is going on as Moon Knight instructs you to climb into the cradle that is suspended underneath it. You do as he says, lying down in what is little more than a harness slung beneath the craft. Then Moon Knight climbs in, lying down beside you.

With Moon Knight's hands on the controls, the craft takes to the air again, propelled by who knows what motive force. In no time at all you are a dizzying height above the city and the whirling flight of the drone soon makes you feel nauseous. You can't quite believe what is happening to you. You are an Egyptologist, not the Falcon! Take **+1 {IN THE HEIGHTS}**.

Make a supernatural senses test. Roll one die, and add your **MYSTIC** and **MIND** to it, and your **{ECLIPSED}**, if you have any. What is the result?

10 or more: turn to **91**.

9 or less: turn to **191**.

43

The [Ankh] is two feet long and very heavy, made as it is from solid gold. It must be worth a king's ransom, but its value to you right now is priceless as you prepare to defend yourself with it, wielding the precious artifact like a club.

The Living Mummy snarls and makes a grab for you, but you bat the horror away.

An almighty crash from above has you looking to the ceiling, and you briefly see a shadowy figure descending amidst glittering glass shards, a crescent-shaped cloak spread out behind it.

The man lands on top of the Mummy, hitting it square in the chest and sending it flying. Take +1 {UNLOCKED}.

Momentum carrying him forward, he turns his landing into a roll, before rising to his feet, all in one smooth action. The figure then turns his attention to you.

"Are you all right?" he asks. His face is covered by a white cloth mask. In fact, your savior's bodyglove, cloak, and cowl are white too, and remind you of the Mummy's bandages.

You stare at the costumed super hero, dumbfounded. "M-moon Knight?"

Turn to **19**.

44

"You'll be in need of a doctor by the time I'm done with you," Moon Knight growls, arming himself with his silver-spiked cesti battle gloves before leaping at the villain. "Or should that be a stonemason?" Take **+1** {UNLOCKED}.

This is a moderate fight.

Round one: roll two dice, add your **MIGHT**, and subtract your {IN THE HEIGHTS}. If the total is 11 or more, you win the first round.

Round two: roll two dice, add your **MIGHT**, and subtract your {IN THE HEIGHTS}. If the total is 10 or more, you win the second round.

If you won the second round, turn to **29**.

If you lost the second round, turn to **270**.

45

As you step through the portal, the vista before you flickers and you feel a lurch, like the sudden drop of a rollercoaster, and stumble to a halt.

The sky is now black, as are the desert sands, and there is no moon hanging in the heavens. With a pop of changing air pressures, the portal blinks out of existence.

What happened? Where are you? Wherever it is, you are trapped here.

You turn to Moon Knight for reassurance... but he's not there! You spin around but all you can see is the endless desert. And that's another strange thing; despite the lack of a light source, you can see clearly for miles in every direction.

You don't know where you are, you don't know where Moon Knight has gone, and you don't know what you are going to do to change any of that. Take +1 {FEARFUL} and -1 MIND.

Your heart is racing, and you start to take deep breaths to bring your rising sense of panic under control. Slowly turning on the spot, you stare at the far horizon, looking for any landmark you could focus on.

And then you see it: an angular structure rising out of the desert, directly beneath the glowing orb of a moon that wasn't there a moment ago. Having no other destination to provide you with any bearings, you head toward it. You trudge over the rippling, midnight dunes until at last you stand before the weathered ruins of a temple from the Age of the Pharaohs.

You realize you are not alone here. Lying on the ground, half-buried by the sand, is a man clad in combat fatigues. He is not moving.

What do you want to do?

Approach the man and check if he's alive: turn to **227**.

Call out to the man: turn to **247**.

Stay where you are and simply observe him for a moment: turn to **265**.

46

"Jack Russell," Moon Knight says, and the Werewolf immediately fixes his gaze on the vigilante. "You know me. We have fought against each other and side by side many times. I am the avatar of Khonshu but this night I bring not the moon god's vengeance but his calming beneficence."

Take **+1 {GRANTED}** and then make an animal mastery test. Roll one die, add your **MYSTIC** to it, and add you **{ECLIPSED}**, if you have any. What's the total?

10 or more: add the ACHIEVEMENT: *The Dog Whisperer*, then turn to **59**.

9 or less: turn to **103**.

47

Loading a bolt into the [Crossbow], you take aim, pull the trigger, and let the projectile fly. You can't miss your target, but the bolt doesn't even make contact, bouncing off the magical shield protecting the Victorian brownstone instead.

Unsurprisingly, Doctor Strange doesn't come to the door. However, the approaching zombie hordes are getting closer all the time.

Take **+1 {NOISY NEIGHBOURS}** then turn to **282**.

48

The Werewolf has Moon Knight pinned to the ground with his savage claws. While he remains incapacitated, the zombie horde closes in.

You watch, utterly unable to help, as Moon Knight is dragged down by the undead horrors. Before they can do the same to you, you see the Fist of Khonshu rise once more, only now transformed into a zombie with a craving for human flesh himself! Appropriately enough, it is Moon Knight who passes on the plague to you.

By morning, New York City will be a new kingdom of the dead.

The End.

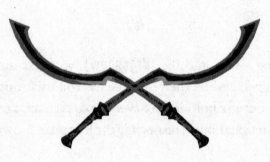

49

Moon Knight does his best, but with one wing half-gone, and the two of you slung beneath it, the drone is all but impossible to maneuver as it goes down. For a moment, it looks like it is going to smash into the side of an apartment building, but at the last second Moon Knight manages to juke it upward and the craft comes down on the roof instead.

Miraculously, it is a crash landing that both of you manage to walk away from, but not without cost to both body and mind. Take **-1 MIGHT** and **-1 MIND**, and **+1 {CRASH LANDING}**.

"How are you, brother?" comes a voice from the top of a nearby water tank. Following the voice to its source, you do a double take when you see what you at first think to be another Moon Knight, except that your companion is still standing on the rooftop next to you.

When you look again more closely, you see that the other's Kevlar body armor is darker, and not just because he is silhouetted against the moon.

Turn to **181**.

50

"Stop!" the Werewolf pants between great panting breaths. "I'm all right now. I won't attack you again."

Turn to **59**.

51

A chemical accident gave French chemist Paul Duval the ability to turn anything to stone, simply by touching it. Do you have anything about you that can defend against the villain's superpower?

> If you have a [Khopesh], and you want to use it now, turn to **35**.
>
> If you have a golden [Ankh], and you want to use that, turn to **15**.
>
> If you want to rely on your wits, turn to **199**.

52

Not knowing how you could make a stand against the animated idol of an ancient Egyptian deity, you turn tail and run. You can feel, as well as hear, the pounding footfalls of the giant as it sets off after you, and your flight becomes a stumbling run as every step the colossus takes sends shockwaves rippling through the ground beneath your feet.

> Turn to **149**.

53

"We mean you no harm," Moon Knight says smoothly, holding his hands up in supplication before the hulking beast.

"Then what bringsss you here?" the alien asks, its voice, which is higher pitched than you would have expected, a mixture of a gurgling gargle and a snake-like hiss.

"New York is under attack. N'Kantu has unleashed a zombie plague upon the city. It isn't safe above ground."

"He'sss done what?" Manphibian exclaims. "There mussst be sssomeone elsssse behind the ssscenesss pulling hisss ssstringsss," the creature goes on.

"What makes you say that?" Moon Knight asks.

"We have fought ssside by ssside in the past as membersss of the Legion of Monssstersss. He hasss even helped policcce Monsssster Metropolisss and keep the more unruly resssidentsss in check."

"So, who do you think is the puppet master?" you ask.

"His dog-headed massster, I sssupossse. Anubisss."

Take +1 {WHO LET THE DOGS OUT?} and +1 MIND.

Moon Knight thanks Manphibian for his help and promises that you will both leave the tunnels as soon as you can. While the creature dives back into the wastewater channel, you and your companion hurry along the rattling walkway.

When you do finally climb another ladder that returns you to the surface, the midnight New York air somehow smells as sweet as you imagine the ancient Egyptian heavenly paradise the Field of Reeds to be.

ACHIEVEMENT: *Going Underground.*

Now turn to **267**.

54

"I don't know what Dr Uraeus is doing here," you mutter under your breath so only the vigilante can hear you, "but if you think about it, this all started when he arranged to have the treasures of King Akharis's tomb put on show at the Metropolitan Museum of Art."

"Then it's time he was made to account for his crimes," your companion – whoever that might be right now – says in that same harsh NYC drawl.

As Moon Knight leaps at Dr Uraeus, the curator throws out a hand and a bolt of black lightning leaps from his fingertips.

If you have the Orb of Belgaroth, turn to **69**.

If not, turn to **20**.

55

"That's one way of putting it," Mr Knight says coldly. "And there's only one approach that works with Black Spectre. I am Khonshu's vengeance made flesh, and there is much I have to avenge when it comes to Carson Knowles."

With that, ignoring the police cordon, Mr Knight sets off down Fifth Avenue on foot. When several officers go to stop him, Detective Flint stands them down. You join the disheveled detective at the barricade the police have set up across the entire width of the road and watch, wondering what Mr Knight intends to do. Take +1 {UNLOCKED}.

You realize that there is someone approaching from the other end of Fifth Avenue. He is dressed in a manner that reminds you of a medieval knight, but one who has joined a biker gang and rides a motorcycle rather than a warhorse. He is armed with a sword and a morning star. As you watch, Mr Knight chooses his own weapons, but what does he pull out from inside his jacket?

Baton: turn to **258**.

Crescent darts: turn to **275**.

Silver cesti: turn to **240**.

56

It is no good – the aggressor is too close, and your warning came too late. A second later, the rocket hits and the drone is sent into a spin by the detonation of the warhead. A cacophony of hazard sirens starts to sound. Over it all you hear Moon Knight call out, "Hold tight and brace for impact! We're going down!"

You had barely taken off before the drone was shot down. Now your life depends on how well Moon Knight can wrestle the drone's controls as the craft plummets out of the sky, its starboard wing destroyed by the rocket.

Make an emergency landing test. Roll one die and add your **MIGHT** and **MIND** to it. What's the result?

Total of 10 or more: turn to **77**.

9 or less: turn to **49**.

57

"23 degrees north, 34 degrees east," you tell Moon Knight's pilot.

"*Mon dieu*, that's in the Akh'ran Highlands!" Frenchie exclaims. "That's where I've just come from!"

"Then you won't have any difficulties taking us there," Moon Knight throws in.

Take **+1 MIND** and the ACHIEVEMENT: *Geography Lesson*.

Now turn to **171**.

58

You drop, and your heart jumps into your throat. Your hair streams in the wind of your passing as the two of you describe an arcing parabola across the void.

And then you touch down again on the other side, stumbling clear of the ledge and only coming to a halt when you are safely inside the other tunnel. Moon Knight tugs the grappling hook free of its anchor point, then winds the cable back into the baton at the flick of a switch.

ACHIEVEMENT: *For Luck.*

Now turn to **98**.

59

The fury has gone from the Werewolf's eyes, and the set of his features and the way he holds himself are now more suggestive of a man than a beast.

"I need answers," Moon Knight tells the cowed creature, "but I also need to know who I am speaking with. Is it Jack Russell or the wolf?"

"It's me, Jack," the lycanthrope confirms.

"Very well. We have fought before but I've never seen you behave in the way you did just now."

What should Moon Knight ask the shapeshifting Jack Russell?

"What came over you?" Turn to **118**.

"What are you doing here?" Turn to **142**.

"Why did you let N'Kantu get away?" Turn to **130**.

You, on the other hand, *do* stop to take a look. Using your extensive knowledge of hieroglyphs and hieratic texts, decoding the script that circles the pillars, or is to be found contained within carved cartouches, you learn that the complex you have entered is dedicated to Seth, the serpent god, and was used by the priesthood of ancient Egypt for the purposes of hiding powerful artifacts, such as the Eye of Horus, as well as to worship their dark master.

Take **+2 {SECRET KNOWLEDGE}** and the ACHIEVEMENT: *Secret Four*.

You wonder what other secret knowledge the hieroglyphs could reveal to you if you had more time to study them. But fearing you will lose Moon Knight if you're not careful, you hurry after him.

You catch up with the vigilante at a T-junction, where the passageway meets another that crosses from left to right, and where he is deliberating which way to go.

"What do you think?" he asks.

How will you answer?

"Left." Turn to **76**.

"Right." Turn to **294**.

"Stained Glass Scarlet!" Moon Knight calls out, clearly recognizing your attacker. "Now is not the time to settle our quarrel. The city is under attack from zombies and its populace is succumbing to their undead plague at a terrifying rate. If you want to fight, fight them!"

As Moon Knight is talking to her, the woman continues to stagger toward your position. The first thing you notice is the crossbow she is holding in one hand, the second is the red gown she is wearing, and the third is her slack-jawed expression and staring pupilless eyes.

The plague is spreading even more quickly than you first thought – Stained Glass Scarlet is already one of the zombies. And she is not alone. More zombies are emerging from side-streets and alleyways and closing on your position.

ACHIEVEMENT: *Code Red.*

This is a boss fight.

Round one: roll two dice and add your **MIGHT** and, if you have any, your {UNLOCKED}. If the total is 15 or more, you win the first round.

Round two: roll two dice and add your **MIGHT** and, if you have any, your {UNLOCKED} and your {ECLIPSED}. If the total is 16 or more, you win the second round.

Round three: roll two dice and add your **MIGHT** and, if you have any, your {UNLOCKED} and your {ECLIPSED}. If the total is 17 or more, you win the third round.

Subtract 1 from the number of rounds you won and adjust your **MIGHT** by that much: this could range from **+2** if you won all three, to **-1** if you lost all three.

If you won round three, turn to **25**.

If you lost round three, Stained Glass Scarlet and the other zombies eventually manage to overwhelm Moon Knight by sheer force of numbers: turn to **107**.

62

Faced by a resurrected ancient Egyptian Mummy, who in their right mind would do anything other than run away? You don't care about where you are running to, only what you are running away from.

ACHIEVEMENT: *Discretion is the Better Part of Valor*.

Not really thinking about where you are going, you find yourself running toward an alabaster statue of Khonshu, the Egyptian god of the moon, and you stumble to a halt, suddenly transfixed. The statue seems to glow in the moonlight bathing it.

The crash of breaking glass from above turns your attention from the statue to the ceiling. A strange figure blots out the moon for a moment as it swoops into the hall, a crescent cloak spread out behind it enabling its graceful descent. Take **+1 {ECLIPSED}**.

The figure lands in a crouch, between you and the lumbering Mummy, before rising to its full height of six feet and two inches. The man turns to you then and you see that his face is covered by a mask. Your savior's bodyglove, cloak, and cowl are all white and glow in the moonlight like the alabaster statue.

"Are you all right?" the figure asks.

But all you can say in reply is, "M-moon Knight?"

Turn to **88**.

63

"All right then," says Moon Knight, "let's see what you've got."

With a roar, Grey Gargoyle springs at the vigilante. Moon Knight dodges out of the way, but his adversary grabs hold of a projecting stone spear, using his own momentum to swing himself around for another go. But as he does so, Moon Knight delivers a powerful kick to the spear he is holding onto. Under the force, the stone shears straight through and the Grey Gargoyle is sent tumbling toward street level.

"That won't keep Duval out of action for long," your companion says, "but we really don't have time to deal with his nonsense on tonight of all nights."

Take +1 {GRANTED}.

Now turn to **106**.

64

Progress slows to a crawl as traffic cops direct you left onto East 54th Street and eventually right onto Park Avenue. As you cruise along the city streets in luxurious style, you peer out of tinted windows at the floodlit skyscrapers.

Many super heroes have their base of operations in New York, not just Moon Knight, and some of them are less secretive about their identities than others. For example, Stark Tower stands on 58th and Broadway like a sentinel watching over the Big Apple, and the Baxter Building on 42nd and Madison is home to the Fantastic Four.

As you eventually make it to the vicinity of Times Square, Mr Knight's patience runs out and he instructs the disembodied "driver" to pull up and park. Getting out of the limousine, you can see the neon glow of the popular tourist destination coming from the other end of the street.

Your companion doesn't exit the vehicle immediately after you, but when he does, he is in the guise of Moon

Knight once more. "We still don't know where N'Kantu actually is, and I don't want to draw unwanted attention to our activities," Moon Knight says, "so I think it best if we approach on foot."

Keeping to secluded corners and alleyways as much as possible, you prepare to enter Times Square. And then you see it, staggering along the alleyway ahead of you, its lumbering gait giving it away immediately. It is N'Kantu the Living Mummy!

"Khonshu be praised!" your companion hisses under his breath and springs forward.

In that instant, something drops from a fire escape above you to land in a lupine crouch between you and Moon Knight, and the Mummy.

You cannot hide your shock and surprise and let out a gasp of horror. The creature is humanoid in form, but his lean, muscular body is covered with a thick layer of fur. His teeth are long and pointed, as are his ears, and his fingernails have grown to become ragged claws. The only concession he has made to clothing is a pair of torn jeans, and they're not ripped in the fashionable way.

First a Mummy and now a Werewolf? You feel you have truly glimpsed beyond the veil this night.

The wolfman's eyes blaze the color of blood and a savage snarl escapes his throat. Meanwhile, N'Kantu is getting away.

If you think Moon Knight should attack the Werewolf, turn to **226**.

If you think Moon Knight should wait to see if the Werewolf makes the first move, turn to **246**.

If you think he should ignore the creature and go after N'Kantu, turn to **268**.

65

Do it, Marc! the voice of Khonshu booms inside your head like the slamming of crypt doors. *You cannot delay. It must be done, and it must be done quickly!*

You watch Moon Knight with anxious eyes as he rocks to and fro, his hands clamped over his ears, wondering what he will do next.

Roll one die. What's the result?

    1-2: turn to **271**.

    3-4: turn to **183**.

    5-6: turn to **146**.

66

You bravely stand your ground as the stone colossus bears down on you, the sickle-shaped sword gripped tightly in both hands. As the idol's stone fingers come within reach, you swing the [Khopesh] at the giant and make contact, the blade scraping across the granite and throwing up a shower of sparks as sword and stone connect.

Despite this, the golden [Khopesh] has no obvious effect on the god-statue. As you prepare to parry the colossus' clutching grasp, it catches the blade between finger and thumb, and snatches the weapon from your grasp.

Strike the [Khopesh] from your Inventory and take +1 {FEARFUL}.

Now turn to **149**.

67

"Doctor Strange, Sorcerer Supreme and Guardian of the Eye of Agamotto," Moon Knight calls out in a loud voice, "we have need of your assistance. Admit us now to your Sanctum Sanctorum before the zombie hordes reach your door!"

As the echoes of the vigilante's words fade, an eerie silence descends over Bleecker Street.

Make a supplication test. Roll one die, and add your **MYSTIC** to it, but deduct any {NOISY NEIGHBOURS} you may have.

9 or more: turn to **234**.

8 or less: turn to **282**.

68

The Werewolf bounds up the steps, overtaking Moon Knight, but rather than leaping on N'Kantu, he suddenly turns and blocks the vigilante's path to his target. The previous wild look has returned to his eyes, and he just manages to snarl an apologetic, "I'm sorry. I cannot resist the power of the Darkhold," before he attacks.

This is a tough fight!

Round one: roll two dice and add your **MIGHT** and, if you have any, your {ABRACADABRA}. If the total is 13 or more, you win the first round.

Round two: roll two dice and add your **MIGHT** and, if you have any, your {ABRACADABRA}. If the total is 14 or more, you win the second round.

If you won the second round, turn to **32**.

If you lost the second round, turn to **48**.

69

The dark energy arcs toward the vigilante, but at the last possible moment it changes direction and is absorbed by the Orb. Take **+1** {ABRACADABRA}.

ACHIEVEMENT: *Now That's Magic!*

"What is the meaning of this?" Dr Uraeus roars, a sibilant hiss behind his words.

Make a threat test. Roll two dice and add your **MYSTIC**, as well as any {DARK POWER} you might have. If you have a [Khopesh] in your Inventory, deduct 1, but if you have an [Ankh], deduct 2 instead, or if you have an [Eye of Horus], deduct 3. What is the final total?

20 or more: turn to **22**.

19 or less: turn to **37**.

70

The Werewolf shakes himself and then, the bestial side of his nature in full control now, he pounces. This is not the first time Moon Knight and the Werewolf have fought, but for all the vigilante's martial arts skills, his feral opponent is unpredictable by nature, and this won't be an easy fight. In fact, this is a boss fight!

Round one: roll two dice and add your **MIGHT** and, if you have any, your {ECLIPSED}. If the total is 13 or more, you win the first round.

Round two: roll two dice and add your **MIGHT** and, if you have any, your {ECLIPSED}. If the total is 14 or more, you win the second round.

Round three: roll two dice and add your **MIGHT** and, if you have any, your {ECLIPSED}. If the total is 15 or more, you win the third round.

Subtract 1 from the number of rounds you won and adjust your **MIGHT** by that much: this could range from +2 if you won all three rounds, to -1 if you lost all three.

If you won at least two rounds, turn to **50**.

If you lost at least two rounds, turn to **30**.

71

You lay the Khopesh on the reading desk so that the Sorcerer might examine it.

"This is a fine weapon indeed," Strange says, a tone of reverence in his voice, as he runs his hands over the sickle-shaped blade. "Not only that, but it is imbued with potent enchantments that would make it particularly effective against undead entities. I don't mean the soulless zombies currently wandering around outside, but true mummies and the ancient dead of other races. In fact, it is such a fine piece that I would be willing to trade something from my collection for it. What do you say?"

If you want to trade the [Khopesh] for something else, turn to **132**.

If you would rather keep hold of it yourself, take **+1 MIGHT** and turn to **297**.

72

The vigilante collides with you and sends you flying. As you hit the ground, you give a grunt of breathless pain. But, as it turns out, it could have been worse. Much worse. That click you heard was a crossbow being shot.

ACHIEVEMENT: *A Close Call.*

Moon Knight quickly rolls off you and gets to his feet. Considering the woman is armed and apparently dangerous, what do you think his next course of action should be?

> Call out and tell the attacker he means her no harm: turn to **61**.
>
> Take the approach that the best form of defense is to attack: turn to **41**.
>
> Flee before she can shoot the crossbow again: turn to **25**.

73

You crack Kraven's [Whip] at the Werewolf, perhaps hoping that it might be imbued with a portion of the Hunter's power, but it isn't. It's just a whip.

Take **-1 MIGHT** and the ACHIEVEMENT: *Russian Roulette.*

Turn to **103**.

74

You snatch up the [Canopic Jar] and hold it out before you in what you hope is a threatening manner. The clay feels strangely warm to the touch and, as you keep your eyes on the Mummy, at the edge of your vision you think you see the hieroglyphs etched into the pot glow redly, as if from within.

A howl of rage issues from the Mummy's desert-dry throat and it lunges for you.

At that moment, an almighty crash from above has you both looking to the ceiling. Something briefly blots out the moon as a figure swoops down into the hall, a crescent cloak spread out behind it enabling its graceful descent. Take **+1 {GRANTED}**.

The figure lands in a crouch, beside the broken sarcophagus, before rising to his full height of six feet and two inches. The man is dressed from head to toe in white, from the expressionless mask covering his face and his armored bodyglove, to his hooded cowl, and the cloak that sweeps down from his shoulders.

"Moon Knight!" you gasp in wonder.

Turn to **260**.

75

"Yes, Mr Knight serves a purpose, but sometimes only Khonshu's true avatar will do. If Black Spectre wants Moon Knight, then that is what he will get. And may he live to regret it."

Take +1 {ECLIPSED}, then turn to **215**.

76

The two of you follow the tunnel as it leads deeper into the bedrock of the mountain. The walls are of dressed stone covered with a layer of plaster, on top of which have been painted scenes of the gods in the most vibrant colors. The passageway is lit by flickering torches, which create the subtle illusion that the painted figures are moving.

Eventually the passageway turns right, and you find yourselves at the entrance to an underground chamber. The floor is tiled with great sandstone slabs and each one bears a different hieroglyph.

Make a decoding test. Roll one die and add your **MIND**, plus any {SECRET KNOWLEDGE} you may have. What's the result?

Total of 9 or more: turn to **173**.

8 or less: turn to **193**.

77

Moon Knight fights with the drone to maintain control as it comes down on top of an apartment building, enabling the two of you to jump free just before it makes impact. The craft gouges a great rut in the flat roof but the two of you are safe, for the time being. Take **+1 {CRASH LANDING}**.

"We meet again, brother," comes a sneering voice from the top of the water tank bolted to the roof. Following the voice to its source, you do a double take when you see what you at first think to be Moon Knight, except that your companion is still standing on the rooftop next to you.

When you look again more closely, you see that the other's Kevlar body armor is darker, and not just because he is silhouetted against the moon.

Turn to **181**.

78

You drop, your heart jumps into your mouth, and you panic. As your body convulses in fear, Moon Knight almost loses his grip on you... almost, but not quite.

And then your terrifying flight across the void is over and you land on the ledge on the other side, but only barely, and the two of you tumble into the mouth of the tunnel beyond.

Moon Knight groans in pain as he picks himself up, rubbing at his side. He has pulled a muscle whilst trying to keep you from falling. Take **-1 MIGHT**.

Moon Knight tugs the grappling hook free of its anchor point, retracting the cable with the flick of a switch, before the two of you set off again in silence.

ACHIEVEMENT: *I Think We Took a Wrong Turn.*

Now turn to **98**.

79

A loud boom rocks the city street, causing cars to swerve and those few onlookers who have gathered to watch the battle between Moon Knight and his adversary to cry out in alarm. Looking in the direction of the sound, you see a smoky fireball rise into the sky.

"Another time, Khonshu's fist!" the Grey Gargoyle shouts, and vanishes into the night.

"Duval will have to wait," Moon Knight says, his tone

as grim as ever. "We have more pressing matters to attend to."

However, the Grey Gargoyle dropped something as he took flight. It is a [Vial of Serum].

Turn to **106**.

80

A tremor passes through the subterranean chamber, almost causing you to lose your footing and sending a shower of sand raining down from above.

"What do we do now?" Moon Knight says, echoing your query. "Now, we run."

The white-clad vigilante leads the way with Frenchie following, adrenaline giving you the spur you need to keep up as Moon Knight leads you back through the temple complex, successfully negotiating the deathtraps that challenged you on the way through the underground complex.

But as you flee through the penumbral gloom of the temple, the tremors continue to shake the tunnels around you, as if Anubis's ritual – or should that be Seth's ritual? – somehow weakened the very structure of the mountain.

Make a speed test. Roll one die, add your **MIGHT** and any {ECLIPSED} you may have. What's the result?

Total of 12 or more: turn to **200**.

11 or less: turn to **150**.

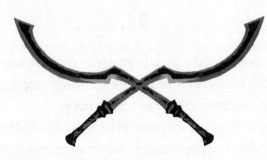

81

"You might well run!" the villain exclaims. "You are pathetic and not worthy of the great Grey Gargoyle's attentions, but I shall minister to you nonetheless."

With that, he leaps after you. Faster and more powerful than you are, the Grey Gargoyle catches up with you within moments. Taking off one of his gloves, he grabs hold of your shoulder. It immediately goes numb. The feeling of numbness spreads and, looking down, you stare in disbelief – your skin and clothes are turning to stone!

Your own flesh becoming gray and pitted like granite is the last thing you ever see, while the look of horror on your face becomes immortalized in stone forever.

The End.

82

Blood – your blood – flies through the air, and a few drops hit the humming canopic jar where it hangs suspended, at the exact center of the pyramidal chamber.

You watch as the crimson plasma is absorbed by the glowing hieroglyphs etched into the container, which begin to glow more brightly. Cracks start to appear in the jar, which pulse with the same fierce red light as the picture script. At the same time, an ear-splitting howl fills the chamber, as if the souls trapped within it are all crying out in unison.

All eyes are on the jar now. The wail increases in intensity, and you are forced to throw your hands over your ears, until, with an incredible *CRACK!* the canopic jar explodes.

All are floored by the bow-wave of pressure, including mighty Anubis himself. The air is filled with a strange mist that whirls about the chamber. Within it you see the fleeting faces again, not screaming in pain but howling with delight, and then they are gone.

"What is going on?" Turning, you see Frenchie Duchamp staggering into the chamber, clearly in a daze. He has managed to free himself from Moon Knight's improvised bindings, but the wild look has gone from his eyes. He appears to be human again.

But the god of the dead, the destruction of the soul-trapping canopic jar, and Frenchie being cured of the zombie plague... none of these are the strangest thing you will witness before your adventure is over.

"What have you done?" screams Dr Uraeus. "We were so close!"

As you watch, the curator seems to swell with anger. But it is more than that... his body is physically increasing in size. First, it is the buttons on his shirt that burst, but before long his suit can no longer contain his swelling form.

But more than changing in size, his body is also changing shape! The man's limbs are taken within the lengthening body, the skin changing color and hardening until it is scaly, like that of a snake. Still he keeps growing. You watch, too terrified to look away, as Dr Uraeus's face elongates, at the same time as his nose flattens, and when he opens his eyelids, you see the ophidian orbs that now lie beneath.

"It is Seth, the serpent god!" Moon Knight declares, raising his voice to be heard over the horrid hissing that is now echoing from the walls of the chamber. "It was he who was behind this all along!"

That may be true, but how can anyone – even a super hero like Moon Knight – fight a god of Heliopolis at the height of his powers?

But you must try something, or in moments you and your companion will both be dead, swallowed alive by the monstrous serpent! So, what's it to be? How will you defend yourself against Seth, the serpent god of death?

Use a [Khopesh], if you have one? Turn to **96**.

Use an [Ankh], if you have one? Turn to **126**.

Use a [Whip], if you have one? Turn to **143**.

Use a [Tactical Grenade], if you have one? Turn to **157**.

Use a [Vial of Serum], if you have one? Turn to **175**.

Use a [Crossbow], if you have one? Turn to **195**.

Use an [Alien Device], if you have one? Turn to **216**.

Use some [Sticks of Dynamite], if you have any? Turn to **239**.

Use an [Eye of Horus], if you have one? Turn to **253**.

Use the [Black Grimoire], if you have it? Turn to **273**.

Use the [Orb of Belgaroth], if you have it? Turn to **290**.

Prepare to fight: turn to **192**.

83

A half-dozen of Moon Knight's crescent darts hit the Manphibian, sending him reeling, and Khonshu's avatar follows up with a final powerful kick to the chest that sends the alien toppling back into the filthy watercourse. Before he can recover himself, the current carries the monster over a waterfall, plunging him into a roaring void.

But the inhuman creature has left something behind. The [Alien Device] looks like a classic ray gun from a black and white sci-fi serial, but with a small parabolic dish at the end of its muzzle.

"We must press on," Moon Knight tells you. "There's not far to go now."

"How do you know?" you challenge him. "Have you used this shortcut before?"

"When you have dedicated your life to bringing vengeance to all those who would threaten those who travel by night, you can't help visiting some very dark places indeed."

And smelly too, or so it seems to you.

When you do finally climb another ladder that returns you to the surface, the midnight New York air is as sweet to you as you imagine the ancient Egyptian heavenly paradise the Field of Reeds to be.

ACHIEVEMENT: *Going Underground.*

Now turn to **267**.

84

You know it is not uncommon for brothers to fight, but you have never witnessed a brotherly battle like this one before. Moon Knight delivers a roundhouse kick to his adversary, followed by a stomach punch, before finishing with an uppercut to the jaw. The Fist of Khonshu has laid his brother out cold. Take **+1 MIGHT**.

You feel a combination of astonishment and fear at observing this. What must have happened for Moon Knight to have such a combative relationship with his brother?

"I will come back and deal with him later, but first we need to deal with N'Kantu," Moon Knight declares.

Turn to **106**.

85

Brandishing the [Ankh] before the colossus, you hope that its innate power will repel the stone giant. Unfortunately, it has no such effect, and the god-statue plucks the artifact from your grasp, crushing it between finger and thumb.

You are left without your talisman, fearing that this may be the end for you.

Strike the [Ankh] from your Inventory and take +2 {FEARFUL}.

Turn to **149**.

86

Moon Knight is suddenly eerily calm, but it is the calm that comes before a storm.

"Anubis must be stopped," he says in the same unnerving drawl. "The sacrifice must be made."

"The sacrifice *must* be made," Khonshu's voice echoes inside your head.

And then, one of his razor-sharp crescent darts gripped tight in his hand, Moon Knight leaps at you and slashes the blade across your throat.

The sacrifice is made, the ritual is disrupted, thanks to the spilling of your blood, but your adventure is over.

ACHIEVEMENT: *The Ultimate Sacrifice*.

Final score: 0 stars.

The End.

87

You hurl the glass vial at the Werewolf and score a direct hit. It breaks, splashing the creature with its chemical contents. The wolfman howls in pain as smoke rises from his fur, and you can see that where the liquid has made contact with his body, his flesh appears to be turning to stone.

But the transmogrifying effect does not affect the rest of the Werewolf's body and now the creature turns his blood-red gaze on you, an animal hatred burning within his lupine eyes.

Strike the [Vial of Serum] from your Inventory and turn to **103**.

Before we continue with the adventure, let's set up the powers for your team of Moon Knight and the Egyptologist. There are three core stats, **MIGHT**, **MYSTIC**, and **MIND**. You remember that from the introduction, which you absolutely read, yeah? Hm.

Might represents Moon Knight's current strength, agility, and resilience. Very helpful for punching things, which will turn out to be useful any moment now, as well as throwing things, leaping over things, breaking things, and all sorts of other tasks you'll encounter in due course.

Mystic is a measure of how persuasive other people consider Moon Knight to be at the time, but it also has a supernatural element to it. It can be affected by events that might impact other people's perceptions, and by acts of god. Any god.

Mind indicates your team's current level of mental ability. It's handy for solving problems, spotting objects that are out of the way or hard to notice and thinking up clever solutions on the fly. However, you'll still have to solve the puzzles in this book on your own.

Your core stats will change repeatedly over the course of your adventure, so you'll need to keep track of them on a piece of paper or something similar. You start with **MIGHT** of 2, **MYSTIC** of 3, and **MIND** of 2.

Right – back to the adventure…

As the vigilante is checking on you, the Living Mummy

flings forward an arm and some of the bandages covering it unravel as it does so. These ribbons of ancient cloth seem to move with a sentience of their own, wrapping themselves around Moon Knight's arms, threatening to pull him to the ground.

Make a strength test. Roll one die and add your **MIGHT** and **MYSTIC** to it. What's the result?

Total of 9 or more: turn to **254**.

8 or less: turn to **133**.

89

Moon Knight attacks Kraven with a flurry of kicks and punches. It seems that years spent hunting big game in Africa, coupled with the effects of the mystical serum that flows through his veins, means that the Russian can not only predict what his attacker's moves will be, but when he does make an error of judgment, he is either quick enough or strong enough to get the better of the vigilante each time.

The fight only comes to an end when the hunter traps Moon Knight in a bear hug before pile-driving him into the ground.

"You are not worthy!" Kraven roars in triumph.

Moon Knight sits up, clearly in pain and short of breath. "It is not me you should have been hunting anyway," he says, dabbing at a bloody patch on his otherwise white mask, where he must have split his lip.

Kraven raises an eyebrow, his curiosity piqued. "You know where the wall-crawler is?"

"No, but I do know that N'Kantu the Living Mummy is loose in the city. A creature that has evaded death for over three thousand years. Now wouldn't that make a fine trophy to hang above your mantelpiece?"

"It would indeed," Kraven muses. "I thank you, Moon Knight, and may the god whom you serve show you mercy despite the dishonor you have done by failing him this night."

With that, the hunter runs off, clearly hoping to catch up with N'Kantu himself. Take **+1** {HUNTED}.

Turn to **298**.

90

Making it to the foot of the steps at last, Moon Knight starts to race up them to reach the Living Mummy and bring an end to his ritual.

If you have a {GOOD DOG} of 1, turn to **68**.

If not, turn to **32**.

91

Moon Knight pilots the drone over the labyrinthine network of streets beneath, heading south toward Times Square, and always on the lookout for N'Kantu the Living Mummy.

You cannot quite believe that you are there beside him, acting as an additional pair of eyes and ears as you gaze down at the city in a way you never have before.

And then, as you cross the southernmost limits of Central Park and head on over Midtown, you suddenly catch sight of a distinctive looking figure, standing on the flat roof of an apartment building. It isn't the Mummy. In fact, it looks like Moon Knight, only the man's costume is darker, and he is perhaps more heavily built.

If you want to alert Moon Knight to the presence of his doppelganger below, turn to **205**.

If you would prefer not to distract him from the task of piloting the drone, turn to **24**.

92

The vigilante collides with you and sends you flying. The two of you hit the ground and give a breathless grunt, but Moon Knight's sounds more pained than yours.

As he struggles to his feet, you see that he has been hit in the thigh by a crossbow bolt! Take **-1 MIGHT**.

"I told you to be *careful*," Moon Knight hisses, in what sounds like annoyance as well as pain.

Considering the woman is armed and apparently dangerous, what do you think his next course of action should be?

Call out and tell the woman he means her no harm: turn to **61**.

Take the approach that the best form of defense is to attack: turn to **41**.

Flee before she can shoot the crossbow again: turn to **25**.

93

"Now that is a potent artifact," Doctor Strange declares as he lays his eyes upon the [Ankh]. "I can feel the power radiating from it. The ankh is a potent symbol of ancient Egypt and appears repeatedly in all manner of magical texts. It is also known as the Key of Life, and this particular talisman will help guard against negative forces and conjurations of dark magic."

"I could have told you that," Moon Knight says. He's not wrong either. After all, you are both experts when it comes to the mythology and beliefs of ancient Egypt.

"I would love to have such a piece form part of my collection," Strange goes on, "if you would be willing to trade."

If you want to trade the [Ankh] for something from

the Sorcerer Supreme's collection, turn to **132**.

If you would rather keep hold of it, take **+1 MYSTIC** and turn to **297**.

94

As Moon Knight watches the road, you rap on the door three times, sending the esoteric wards racing across the surface of the shimmering magical shield in flashes of rippling green light.

Make a summoning test. Roll one die and add your **MYSTIC** and your **MIGHT**, but deduct any {NOISY NEIGHBOURS} or {DARK POWER} you may have.

10 or more: turn to **234**.

9 or less: turn to **282**.

95

"Black Spectre," Moon Knight replies, "also known as Carson Knowles, a seriously disturbed man with a grudge against the city. We've had our run-ins in the past, but he just doesn't seem to know when to stay dead."

Take +1 {GRANTED}.

"We need to do something and fast," Detective Flint says, "before he triggers that bomb."

"Are you sure he really has planted a bomb somewhere nearby?" you ask. "Or could he be bluffing?"

"It's possible but unlikely," says Mr Knight. "This is Black Spectre, after all. He doesn't make idle threats."

"Well…" you begin.

> "If Moon Knight has taken him down before, I'm sure he could again." Turn to **215**.

> "I'm sure a rich crime fighter like you has some impressive tech he could use in a situation like this." Turn to **3**.

96

The [Khopesh] will be of more use in the hands of a skilled fighter like Moon Knight, so you throw it to him. He deftly catches it by the hilt and makes a trial slash with the weapon, the golden blade shining as brightly as the sun in the inconstant light that illuminates the subterranean vault.

Take +1 MIGHT and +1 {SNAKEBITE} and cross the [Khopesh] off your Inventory. You may not select this option again.

Do you have anything else you could bring to bear against the Serpent God?

If you do, turn back to **82** and choose an option you haven't tried already.

If not, it is time Khonshu's avatar exacted the Moon God's vengeance against the Serpent God: turn to **192**.

97

As is evident from what you have experienced here, as long as the canopic jar remains in the hands of N'Kantu, the zombie plague will never be contained. So, turning his back on his friend, Moon Knight makes for the opening in the bottom of the looming cliff face, with you following at his heels.

As the two of you climb the excavated steps that lead to the entrance, a strangled cry has you both turning to witness a terrible sight. A zombie appears to have come out of nowhere from behind an abandoned jeep, taking Frenchie by surprise. A shot rings out, but the Frenchman clearly missed, as in the next moment he falls to the ground with the zombie on top of him, and the horror's teeth sunk into his neck, as if it is giving him a love bite.

Moon Knight looks like he is about to go back and help his friend until you put out your hand and say, "It's too late. You can't do anything for him now. You know that."

The vigilante lets out a bellow of rage and frustration before turning back toward the entrance to the temple and storming inside.

ACHIEVEMENT: *French Kissing*.

From the entrance, a short passageway leads to a vast hypostyle hall. You gaze in wonder. Sixty towering pillars, carved to look like papyrus stems, disappear into the darkness above. But Moon Knight doesn't stop to take in the intricate carvings that cover the numerous columns.

Following him, for fear of getting left behind, the two of you soon come to a T-junction.

"Which way, do you think?" he asks.

How will you answer?

"Left." Turn to **76**.

"Right." Turn to **294**.

98

Leaving the chamber behind you, you turn another corner and find yourselves proceeding along yet another long, torchlit passageway. However, halfway along it a doorway opens onto another chamber, and you immediately know this is the way you must go.

The chamber is actually no more than a processional gallery, at the end of which stands an ornately carved gateway. Light spills from the far chamber, illuminating the statues that line the processional way in rippling waves of crimson, purple, and ultramarine.

There can be no doubt that the ritual you have come all this way to stop is being conducted within that chamber. But, as you enter the gallery, you hesitate.

It has been both a dream and a nightmare to join Moon Knight on this quest. But could your presence at his side be more than simple circumstance?

"Why am I here?" you ask your companion.

"What? You're asking me this now?" Moon Knight hisses.

"It's because Khonshu thinks I'm some mysterious high priest, isn't it?" you go on.

Moon Knight lets out a heavy sigh. "Khonshu believes you are a scion of an ancient bloodline, descended from the priesthood of ancient Egypt. Your distant ancestor was one of those who stood up to Akharis the Accursed and ensured that his evil plans were thwarted. Rather than gain eternal life, Akharis was put into the ground and forgotten about for centuries."

"Until now," you say.

"Until now."

An awkward silence descends between you.

"All right then," you decide at last, "let's do this."

And so the two of you advance through the gallery, past the colossal, carved, animal-headed figures, keeping to the shadows between them, so as not to alert anyone in the ritual chamber to your presence.

Which of the following is highest?

Your {DARK POWER}: turn to 117.

Your {ABRACADABRA}: turn to 137.

Your MYSTIC: turn to 167.

99

The battle is brutal, with Manphibian's alien physiology granting him superhuman strength which he uses to good effect to withstand Moon Knight's martial arts maneuvers. Even Moon Knight's crescent darts are turned aside by the creature's razor-sharp claws.

However, one of them hits a curious alien device Manphibian is carrying. The object looks like a classic ray gun from a black and white sci-fi serial, but with a small parabolic dish at the end of its muzzle. But when the dart hits the device, it somehow activates it.

A cataclysmic wave of sound immediately bursts from the weapon, the concussive waves sending everyone reeling, including Manphibian. You throw your hands over your ears while the creature hisses in pain and dives back into the sewer, vanishing beneath the turbid waters. At the same moment, the cacophonous wail is cut off.

"We don't have a moment to lose," Moon Knight shouts as he grabs you by the hand, but even then, you can barely hear him over the ringing in your ears. "Let's get out of here!"

When you do finally climb another ladder that returns

you to the surface, the midnight New York air is somehow as sweet as you imagine the ancient Egyptian heavenly paradise the Field of Reeds to be.

ACHIEVEMENT: *Wall of Sound.*

Now turn to **267**.

100

Mr Knight, who is sitting next to you in silence, with his fingers steepled before his masked face, suddenly breaks the silence, instructing the disembodied "driver" to go to the corner of 51st and Madison and pull up there.

ACHIEVEMENT: *Secret Two.*

Five minutes later, you are getting out of the limousine and find yourself looking up at the towering gothic edifice of St Patrick's Cathedral. You might not be enjoying a view of the building's grand facade, but it is equal parts impressive and imposing, nonetheless.

Your companion doesn't exit the vehicle immediately after you, but when he does, he is in the guise of Moon Knight once more. "My eyes in the sky have informed me that Fifth Avenue is closed off from 54th through 52nd Street, but we'll be able to see what's going on better from up there." He indicates the twin spires that rise above Fifth Avenue.

"We?" you ask, not sure that you heard him correctly.

"That's right," Moon Knight says as he takes out his baton and prepares to launch the grappling hook built into it at a flying buttress. "Khonshu said that we were to stick together, so we stick together."

How do you want to respond?

> "Well, I suppose there has to be a first time for everything." Turn to **114**.
>
> "No way! You're not taking me up there!" Turn to **161**.

101

As you stumble away from the advancing Mummy, you bump into one of the glass cabinets that dot the exhibition space. Behind the glass, held within two rubber clasps, you see a golden, sickle-shaped sword.

You only hesitate for a moment before shoving the cabinet over. It hits the marble floor with a resounding crash, and you rescue the [Khopesh] from among the shards of broken glass.

Gripping the sword in one shaking hand, you nonetheless hold it out in front of you, in what you hope is a suitably threatening manner. The Living Mummy looks from the glittering blade to you, fixing you with a furious glare that seems to say, "How dare you, a mere mortal, threaten me?"

Regardless, you raise the sword above your head, ready to strike, should the Mummy come one step closer.

An almighty crash has you looking to the ceiling, and you catch a glimpse of a shadowy shape silhouetted against the moon as it smashes through a skylight and drops into the exhibition hall. A crescent-shaped cloak spreads out behind him helping to control his descent, the man hits the Living Mummy in the chest with both feet, and your bandaged assailant is sent flying. Take +1 {UNLOCKED}.

Having landed, the figure turns to you then and you see that his face is covered by a white cloth mask. In fact, your savior's bodyglove, cloak, and cowl are white too, and remind you of the Mummy's bandages.

"Are you all right?" the man asks in a gruff voice.

"M-moon Knight?" you gasp in amazement.

Turn to **19**.

102

It is hard to tell because the woman is in silhouette, but as you watch she appears to raise something in one hand. You hear a click and Moon Knight shouts, "Look out!"

Make a dodge test. Roll one die and add your **MIGHT**.

If the total is 10 or more, turn to **72**.

If the total is 9 or less, turn to **92**.

103

The Werewolf gives voice to a blood-chilling howl, the bestial side of his nature in total control now, and attacks. This is not the first time Moon Knight and the Werewolf have fought, but for all the vigilante's martial arts mastery, his feral opponent is unpredictable by nature and overcoming him won't be easy.

This is a boss fight!

Round one: roll two dice and add your **MIGHT** and, if you have any, your {**ECLIPSED**}. If the total is 15 or more, you win the first round.

Round two: roll two dice and add your **MIGHT** and, if you have any, your {**ECLIPSED**}. If the total is 14 or more, you win the second round.

Round three: roll two dice and add your **MIGHT** and, if you have any, your {**ECLIPSED**}. If the total is 13 or more, you win the third round.

Subtract 1 from the number of rounds you won and

adjust your **MIGHT** by that much: this could range from +2 if you won all three, to -1 if you lost all three.

If you won at least two rounds, turn to **50**.

If you lost at least two rounds, turn to **30**.

104

Having spent almost your entire academic career studying the secrets of the ancient Egyptian pharaohs, and more recently the treasures recovered from the Tomb of Akharis the Accursed, you know many of the spells of the Book of the Dead. One of these is the Opening of the Portals, which you recite in the original Ancient Egyptian.

As you do so, a crimson light ripples across the spell-shield protecting the building, each of the esoteric sigils flaring in turn with each verse of the spell you recite.

Take **+1 MYSTIC** and **+1 {ABRACADABRA}**.

ACHIEVEMENT: *Scholar*.

Now turn to **234**.

The two of you take stock in the aftermath of N'Kantu's escape. The exhibition is ruined but, more importantly, the Living Mummy took the jackal-headed canopic jar of King Akharis with him.

"I must catch up with N'Kantu and get it back," Moon Knight says of the artifact, clearly frustrated, and makes to go after the undead thief.

A booming voice, like the slamming of crypt doors, echoes through the museum's Egyptian gallery, halting the hero in his steps. *Wait, my son!*

Awestruck, you find your eyes drawn to the statue of Khonshu that looks over the exhibition space. Moonlight bathes the alabaster, making it glow so brightly that you have to squint, and for a fleeting second, you imagine that you see not the carved face of a man but a fleshless, avian skull.

Take the high priest with you, the voice continues, *for you will both have your part to play in bringing this servant of Anubis to heel before the night is through.*

Turn to **36**.

106

You make it at last to the vicinity of Times Square. As you still don't know where N'Kantu actually is, and not wanting to draw unwanted attention to your activities or panic the public, Moon Knight decides it would be best if you approach on foot, keeping to secluded corners and alleyways as much as possible.

As you do so, you seize the chance to ask Moon Knight something that has been on your mind ever since you first met: "What ritual are we trying to stop and why did Khonshu refer to me as the 'high priest'?"

You know that the higher-ranking members of the priesthood of ancient Egypt were called the first servants of the gods, such was their importance within society. Their duties included studying and writing hieroglyph texts and training new recruits, as well as performing many of the routine duties associated with the temple. These involved clothing, feeding, and even putting to bed the sculpted images that represented the deity to whom the sanctuary was dedicated. In mortuary temples dedicated to Anubis, priests conducted similar ceremonies to nourish the soul, or "ka," of a deceased pharaoh. But you've never done anything like that.

Your companion takes a moment to answer. "The truth is, I do not know the nature of the ritual N'Kantu seeks to perform, but since it involved him stealing one of the treasures of Akharis the Accursed it cannot be anything good. As to why he called you the high priest–"

Before Moon Knight can finish his sentence, you both catch sight of something staggering along the alley ahead of you. Its lumbering gait gives it away immediately. It is N'Kantu the Living Mummy!

"The Moon be praised!" your companion hisses under his breath and springs forward.

In that instant, something drops from a fire escape above you and lands in a lupine crouch between you and Moon Knight, and the Mummy.

You cannot hide your shock and surprise, and gasp. The creature is humanoid in form, but his muscular body is covered with a thick layer of fur. His teeth are long and pointed, as are his ears, and his fingernails have grown to become ragged claws. The only concession he has made to clothing is a pair of torn jeans, and they're not ripped in the fashionable way.

First a Mummy and now a Werewolf? You feel you have truly glimpsed beyond the veil this night.

The wolfman's eyes blaze the color of blood and a savage snarl escapes his throat. Meanwhile, N'Kantu is getting away.

If you think Moon Knight should attack the Werewolf, turn to **226**.

If you think Moon Knight should wait to see if the Werewolf makes the first move, turn to **246**.

If you think he should ignore the creature and go after N'Kantu, turn to **268**.

107

You watch, utterly unable to help, as Moon Knight is dragged down by the zombies. Before they can do the same to you, you see the Fist of Khonshu rise once more, only now transformed into an undead horror with a craving for human flesh! Appropriately enough, it is Moon Knight who passes on the plague to you. By morning, New York City will be a necropolis, home only to the dead.

ACHIEVEMENT: *City of the Dead*.

The End.

108

Moon Knight dodges another lash from the hunter's whip and smashes Kraven in the side of the head with a Kevlar-padded elbow. The Russian reels and before he can recover himself, Moon Knight follows up with a powerful uppercut that drops the villain on the ground hard.

"You are certainly not worthy of the Fist of Khonshu," Moon Knight tells Kraven, as he ties the hunter's arms behind his back using one of his own leather straps.

Picking up Kraven's [Whip], he offers it to you. "To the victor the spoils. Now let's get cracking."

There is no time to report the apprehension of Kraven the Hunter to the authorities. N'Kantu is still out there somewhere in the city, with the canopic jar he stole from the ancient Egyptian exhibition.

Turn to **298**.

109

Why do you delay, my son? Khonshu demands. *Do it now, Jake. Make the sacrifice!*

"No!" Moon Knight roars, the NYC drawl gone. "Not Jake. Marc! And I know what must be done, but not like this!"

Take **+1 MIND**.

With that, he raises a hand holding one of his crescent darts and leaps at you. As you raise your hands to protect yourself, the dart's razor edge slashes across your outstretched palms.

Turn to **82**.

110

In the face of Moon Knight's fury, N'Kantu beats a hasty retreat, snatching up the canopic jar once more and muttering something under his breath. The spiraling winds rise to a hurricane force in an instant and you struggle to find something to hang onto, lest you are carried away by the magical gale.

You struggle to keep your eyes open in the face of the wind, but you nonetheless catch a glimpse of the portal that opens at the heart of the hurricane. One moment the Mummy is there, the next he has gone. But before Moon Knight can follow him through, the wind drops and the portal closes with a thunderclap of dropping air pressure that makes your ears pop.

N'Kantu, the agent of Anubis, has escaped and taken the cursed canopic jar of Akharis with him.

Turn to **10**.

111

Depressing the trigger button with barely a thought, you hurl the grenade at the colossus. The explosive device sails through the air and strikes the giant's stone torso at the same moment as it detonates.

There is a concussive bang. Instinctively, you turn away and throw your hands over your ears. When you dare to look back, you see that the statue has been rocked by the explosion but, other than a slight indentation in its chest where a piece of granite has cracked and fallen off, it appears unharmed. Is there nothing that can stop this colossus?

As the giant reaches for you again, you fear that this is the end for you.

Strike the [Tactical Grenade] from your Inventory and take +2 {FEARFUL}.

Turn to **149**.

112

"They won't be troubling anyone else," Moon Knight says as he wipes the jackals' blood from his hands.

You turn away, unable to stomach the savagery you were witness to, and fight to stop the gorge rising in your throat.

"There's nothing more to be done here," your companion says. "We still have to catch N'Kantu before he can use the canopic jar."

Leaving the zoo again, the two of you follow a path that leads toward a line of trees that have lost all definition in the darkness, beneath which even darker shadows have gathered.

Turn to **204**.

113

"Tell me everything you can about the artifact," Strange says, "and do not omit even the smallest, most apparently insignificant detail."

And so, you tell him about how the canopic jar was stolen from the museum, and that it was originally recovered from the tomb of the forgotten pharaoh Akharis, and how the hieroglyphs etched into the clay glowed an infernal red when the Living Mummy performed the ritual that unleashed the Tenth Plague of Egypt on New York.

"I have read of this Akharis," Doctor Strange says when you have finished. "It is said that he worshipped Seth above all other gods and built a hidden temple dedicated to the serpent god inside a mountain. That was where the power of the evil one was focused."

"Do you know where this temple was located?"

"Legend tells that it was in what is now known as the Al Shalateen Desert."

"Of course!" Moon Knight exclaims. "The Akh'ran Highlands."

Take **+1 MIND** and **+1 {ABRACADABRA}** and make a note of the GPS coordinates for the Akh'ran Highlands, which are 23°00'00.0" North, 34°00'00.0" East.

Turn to **297**.

114

Not knowing what else to do, you hang on for dear life as Moon Knight puts one arm around you and depresses a button that causes the baton to retract the grappling cable, sending you hurtling skyward.

You dare not look down as the city street dwindles beneath you and stifle a cry at the wind rushing into your face. And then the impression of flight ceases, and you dare to open your eyes again, only to immediately wish you hadn't.

You are standing at the edge of a parapet among the projecting stonework of the cathedral roof, with nothing between you and a far too high drop but a narrow, cracked, and weathered stone balustrade. Take **+1 {IN THE HEIGHTS}**.

"Stay here," Moon Knight instructs you, clearly not realizing that you have no intention of going anywhere right now, and scrambles even higher up to get a better view of Fifth Avenue.

Make an awareness test. Roll one die and add your **MIND** to it.

8 or more: turn to **248**.

7 or less: turn to **262**.

115

"I believe we have found the place Khonshu commanded us to seek out," Moon Knight says, "but, as the instrument of his vengeance, I cannot simply stand by while the agents of Anubis remain at large. Besides, Frenchie is a loyal friend."

He turns to you, his white mask impassive. "What do you think I should do?"

How do you want to respond?

"Help your friend." Turn to **151**.

"Leave him." Turn to **97**.

116

Moon Knight knocks the device out of the villain's grip and the two of them then engage in hand-to-hand combat to see, once and for all, which of them is the stronger. Or is it a case of which of them is the more driven?

This is a boss fight.

Round one: roll two dice and add your **MIGHT** and, if you have any, your {UNLOCKED}. If the total is 13 or more, you win the first round.

Round two: roll two dice and add your **MIGHT** and, if you have any, your {UNLOCKED} and your {ECLIPSED}. If the total is 14 or more, you win the second round.

Round three: roll two dice and add your **MIGHT** and, if you have any, your {UNLOCKED} and your {ECLIPSED}. If the total is 15 or more, you win the third round.

Subtract 1 from the number of rounds you won and adjust your **MIGHT** by that much: this could range from **+2** if you won all three, to **-1** if you lost all three.

If you won two or more rounds, turn to **136**.

If you lost two or more rounds, Black Spectre manages to retrieve the device he was holding: turn to **156**.

117

Feeling a prickling on your skin, you look up and discover that you are standing at the feet of a statue of Sobek, the crocodile god. While Sobek is a river god, he is also a deity who demonstrates great physical prowess and likes his devotees to do the same.

Take +1 MIGHT.

Turn to 187.

118

"There is dark magic at work," whimpers the Werewolf. "I sense the power of the Darkhold behind whatever is happening here."

"The Darkhold?" you ask.

"A book of evil spells," Moon Knight explains.

"And the source of my curse," adds Jack.

"What do you mean?" you ask the wolfman.

"My father acquired a copy of the Darkhold, which includes the secret origin of lycanthropy. Through reading that particular passage he became a werewolf, and I inherited his curse when I turned eighteen. Whenever I am in the presence of that foul grimoire's power, I am at risk of losing control of my wolf form altogether."

Take +1 {ABRACADABRA}.

There is still more to be learned here, and Moon Knight still has questions for the wolfman.

What should he ask next?

"What are you doing here?" Turn to **142**.

"Why did you let N'Kantu escape?" Turn to **286**.

119

Moon Knight summons a craft large enough to carry both of you, although admittedly you are slung underneath it in a harness, and you are soon soaring over Manhattan, as chaos consumes the city below. You can see the zombies piling through the streets and hear the panicked screams of those who have yet to succumb to the rapidly spreading plague, even from up here.

Take **+1 {IN THE HEIGHTS}** and the ACHIEVEMENT: *Take Flight*.

"What's that?" you ask, pointing south. Despite the ever-present light pollution that results in a constant glow over the city at night, you can see the top of what appears to be a bubble of kaleidoscopic light in the vicinity of Greenwich Village.

"Of course!" your companion exclaims. "There is one person in New York who might be better prepared than anyone else to help us halt the spread of this zombie plague – and he lives in a neighborhood on the west side of Lower Manhattan."

"And who is that?" you ask.

"Doctor Stephen Strange, of course."

Turn to **267**.

120

There are simply too many zombies, and they overwhelm you and Moon Knight, closing in on you with snapping teeth and pupilless stares.

If you have an [Ankh], in a last ditch attempt to save the two of you, you wave it at the zombies and the undead horrors immediately recoil, hissing in agitation: turn to **90**.

If you do not have an [Ankh], turn to **107**.

121

You brandish the sickle-shaped sword before the Werewolf and see it glittering in the creature's burning gaze. The effect is almost instantaneous.

Turn to **103**.

122

"What do you mean, you're Stephen?" you ask, deeply unsettled by what is going on.

"There isn't time to explain now, I just need you to trust me," he rails, stepping toward you, a crescent dart in his hand.

But you are not alone within the chamber, and those whom you would seek to thwart have their own pieces to play in the greater game.

Make a threat test. Roll two dice and add your **MYSTIC**, as well as any {**DARK POWER**} you might have. If you have a [**Khopesh**] in your Inventory, deduct 1, but if you have an [**Ankh**], deduct 2 instead, or if you have an [**Eye of Horus**], deduct 3. What is the final total?

20 or more: turn to **22**.

19 or less: turn to **37**.

123

As you take a step toward the woman, you hear a click at the same time as Moon Knight shouts, "Look out!" and bodily bowls into you.

Turn to **92**.

124

You hold up the [**Ankh**] in front of the baroque grand entrance to the brownstone. You can feel the power radiating from it. It is as if the artifact is a tuning fork attuned to the vibrations of the spell-shield protecting the Sanctum Sanctorum.

Take **+1 MYSTIC** then turn to **234**.

125

Moon Knight reels before N'Kantu's onslaught. Having caught up with the Mummy at last, he is determined not to let Anubis's agent get away. But before the vigilante can catch his breath, N'Kantu snatches up the canopic jar once more, and mutters something under his breath. The spiraling winds rise to a hurricane force in an instant and you struggle to find something to hang onto, lest you be carried away by the magical zephyrs.

Struggling to keep your eyes open due to the ferocity of the howling gale, nonetheless you witness a portal open at the eye of the storm. One moment N'Kantu the Living Mummy is there, the next he has gone. The wind drops and the portal snaps shut with a clap of thunder that makes your ears pop.

"Khonshu!" Moon Knight rages in frustration. "Why have you forsaken me?"

Take **-1 MYSTIC** and **-1 {ECLIPSED}**.

N'Kantu, the agent of Anubis, has escaped and taken the cursed canopic jar of Akharis with him.

Turn to **10**.

126

Taking out the [Ankh], you brandish it before the monstrous serpent. The golden artifact feels warm in your hands. The colossal creature hisses and recoils, or so it seems to you. Wielding the [Ankh] fills you with confidence and you begin to believe that you and Moon Knight might yet prevail against the transformed Dr Uraeus.

Take **+1 MYSTIC** and **+1 {SNAKEBITE}** and make a note that you cannot choose this option a second time.

Do you have anything else you could bring to bear against the Serpent God?

If you do, turn back to **82** and make another choice, trying something you haven't attempted before.

If not, it is time to fight: turn to **192**.

127

"Who is this that you speak of?" the Russian asks.

"N'Kantu the Living Mummy," Moon Knight replies, "a creature that has evaded death for over three thousand years. Now wouldn't that be worthy prey for Kraven the Hunter?"

"It would indeed," Kraven muses. "I thank you, Moon Knight. Tonight you live, although I am sure we will meet again one day."

With that, the hunter runs off, clearly hoping to catch up with N'Kantu before you can. Take **+1 {HUNTED}**.

"There will be a reckoning between the Fist of Khonshu and Sergei Kravinoff one day," Moon Knight muses as he watches the villain depart, but makes no move to stop him, "but this night I have prey of my own to hunt."

Turn to **298**.

128

The gigantic serpent convulses in its death throes, only it doesn't die. Instead, it shrinks rapidly, assuming a humanoid form. But this humanoid form isn't that of your boss from the museum, Dr Uraeus. It is that of a man, similar to Anubis in height and build. Rather than wearing nothing more than a loincloth, he is clad in some form of close-fitting scaled armor. His human-seeming head is adorned with a headdress that makes it look like his face is emerging from a hooded cobra's mouth, and he only has one hand.

This is Seth's true form. As he lies there, beaten into submission, the god of the dead steps forward and, seizing hold of him with one powerful hand, Anubis hauls him off the ground.

"I have been deceived," he growls. "And now the deceiver must pay! No one makes a fool of Anubis, so now he must suffer the consequences for daring to think otherwise!"

It is quite clear to you that it was Seth who was manipulating Anubis's actions from behind the scenes for his own ends, whatever those ends may have been. And now he has earned the ire of the god of the dead, he must face the consequences.

"We shall return to the Othervoid and there Seth will be tried by a court of his fellow gods at Celestial Heliopolis."

At Anubis's behest, a portal opens. Through it you can see the bright pinpricks of stars and galaxies set against the oblivion black of deep space. Drifting within this cosmic void is what appears to be a temple city, comprised of great pyramids, shrines, and other structures. But closer than that, between the space-borne necropolis and the yawning portal, you make out a grand barque that sails closer with every passing second. It is just such a one as would have carried dead pharaohs from the mortuary temples of Luxor across the Nile to the West Bank and to their final resting place in the Valley of the Kings.

The great boat, steered by a hawk-headed helmsman, comes close enough for Anubis to step through the portal and straight onto its deck, dragging the shamed serpent god with him.

The curious interstellar vessel sets off once again across the void, on the return journey to Celestial Heliopolis, and the portal starts to shrink. Before it closes altogether Anubis turns and acknowledges you both with a nod of the head and you hear him say, "Farewell, Avatar of Khonshu. We will meet again... but not too soon, I trust."

The door between dimensions closes, leaving you and Moon Knight, and a confused-looking Frenchie Duchamp, alone within the Darkhold-inscribed ritual chamber. There is no sign of N'Kantu. The Living Mummy must have fled the accursed temple already.

"What do we do now?" you ask Moon Knight.

"Now we must retrace our steps and leave this place. There is nothing for us here anymore."

If you have a combined **MIND** and **{ABRACADABRA}** of 10 or more, turn to **300**.

If not, but you have a combined **MYSTIC** and **{ECLIPSED}** and **{UNLOCKED}**] of 15 or more, turn to **250**.

If neither of these options are available to you, turn to **80**.

129

Moon Knight and N'Kantu trade blows, the undead horror blocking the hero's karate kicks with his sinewy arms. At the same time, the Mummy tries to lay his hands on Moon Knight so that he can either swing him against one of the stone statues on display in the exhibition or throttle the life from him.

With your back to the balcony that overlooks the entrance hall below, you watch as N'Kantu makes a lunge for the vigilante. Moon Knight drops, avoiding the flailing arms, and delivers a punch to the stomach. As the Living

Mummy doubles up and staggers backward, the hero rises and follows it up with a two-handed blow to the solar plexus.

N'Kantu reels under the barrage of blows. You are so taken up with the fight, you barely register the fact that the Mummy is coming closer with every staggered step until he turns and gives you a powerful shove. You can do nothing to save yourself as you go over the balcony backward and drop toward the solid stone floor twenty feet below. Take +1 {IN THE HEIGHTS}.

What happens next only takes a matter of seconds, but it feels much longer to your racing brain. As you fall, Moon Knight lunges past the Living Mummy and dives over the parapet after you. Even as he swoops toward you, his cloak acting like a hang-glider, he takes hold of what looks like a white baton and presses a switch. A grappling hook fires from the end of the baton and Moon Knight grabs hold of you, just as the hook finds purchase somewhere among the roof lights, arresting your fall and depositing you safely on the floor below.

You feel understandably shaken after such a close call, but, nonetheless, you follow Moon Knight as he runs back up the stairs to the exhibition gallery, only to discover that while he was busy saving your life, the Living Mummy has escaped.

Turn to **105**.

130

"I didn't!" the wolfman snarls. "At least, that wasn't my intention."

"I thought you might be working together," says Moon Knight.

"Just because we were in the Legion of Monsters together? Talk about stereotyping! I had no idea N'Kantu was back in town, never mind why."

Take **+1 {HAPPY HALLOWEEN}**.

What should Moon Knight ask next?"

"What are you doing here?" Turn to **142**.

"What came over you?" Turn to **23**.

131

The battle is over, but it served its purpose. The Living Mummy has made his escape. As the exhausted jackals slink away into the night, there is nothing to be done but resume your pursuit of N'Kantu. Take **-1 MIGHT**.

Leaving the zoo again, the two of you follow a path that leads toward a line of trees that have lost all definition in the darkness, and beneath which even darker shadows have gathered.

Turn to **204**.

132

Doctor Strange scours the shelves of his magical library and finally settles upon two items that he is willing to part with but that he thinks may also be of use to you.

"This is the Black Grimoire," he says, placing a large, leatherbound tome on the reading desk. Its cover has blackened with age, while the book is held shut with two heavy silver clasps. "It is a book of spells from Pendle, in the north of England. The conjurations and enchantments it contains are not to be trifled with, but sometimes the best way to fight fire is with fire."

Leaving the tome where it is, Strange summons a crystal ball from a high shelf, which obligingly comes to rest on the palm of one outstretched hand.

"This is the Orb of Belgaroth that I recovered from the ruins of the fortress of Caer Skaal. It is able to absorb dark magic. So, which is it to be?"

Strike the item you are giving up from your Inventory and make your choice.

If you want to take the **[Black Grimoire]**, turn to **201**.

If you want to exchange your item for the **[Orb of Belgaroth]**, turn to **220**.

Moon Knight fights to break free of the Mummy's constricting bandages but it is not enough. The hero is suddenly yanked backward and hurled across the hall by the Mummy's supernatural strength, only coming to a halt when he collides with a hieroglyph-inscribed obelisk. Take **-1 MIGHT**.

What the Mummy does next surprises you. Rather than continue his battle with Moon Knight, he turns his attentions to the exhibits. Hurling one of the glass cabinets to the ground, he plucks something from amidst the wreckage before fleeing the hall with his prize. But what could the Living Mummy want with a dusty canopic jar?

Turn to **105**.

134

You have trusted Moon Knight this far, so why not now as well? Even if he has changed his name to Stephen for some reason.

But you are shaken from your bewildered stupor when the vigilante takes one of this razor-sharp crescent darts and slashes its tip across the palm of your open hand.

You pull it back, in surprise as much as pain, but the sacrifice has already been made. Moon Knight immediately releases his hold on you and flicks the blood that has collected on the blade into the air.

Turn to **82**.

135

You watch, utterly helpless, as Moon Knight is dragged down by the undead archaeologists and zombified local labor force. Before they can do the same to you, you see the Fist of Khonshu rise once more – only now he is transformed into an undead horror with a craving for human flesh! Appropriately enough, it is Moon Knight who passes on the plague on to you.

By tomorrow morning, the Earth will be a dead world inhabited by nothing but gods and monsters.

The End.

136

Black Spectre is no longer a threat to either the vigilante or the city. As the cops hurry to secure the criminal, Moon Knight is free to examine the device the villain was holding. It is a [Tactical Grenade]. Either it is equipped with a delayed trigger or Black Spectre was intending to kill both himself and Moon Knight with the explosive device.

As the realization of what the villain was prepared to do begins to sink in, you feel your blood turn cold. What a chilling plan!

Turn to **206**.

137

You suddenly have the most vivid feeling that someone is watching you. Looking up, you see that you are standing beneath a statue of the ibis-headed god Thoth, the master of knowledge, giver of language, and patron of scribes. In that instant, a measure of Thoth's wisdom is passed to you.

Take **+1 MIND** and **+1 {ABRACADABRA}**.

Turn to **187**.

138

"N'Kantu has the knowledge of centuries to draw upon and was a powerful fighter, of almost superhuman power, even before he was turned into an indestructible Mummy," says Moon Knight, "so perhaps direct combat is not the most effective way to overcome him."

What do you think Moon Knight should use to defeat the Living Mummy?

A [Whip], if you have one: turn to **153**.

A [Tactical Grenade], if you have one: turn to **166**.

A [Vial of Serum], if you have one: turn to **237**.

His usual Khonshu-consecrated weapons and martial arts skills: turn to **13**.

139

Moon Knight deftly jinks the crescent-shaped craft out of the way and the rocket hurtles past, missing the drone by mere inches before smashing into a skyscraper behind you.

He turns the drone toward the figure on the rooftop, clearly intent on delivering his vengeance to this knight of shadows. Rather than fire another missile at you, the man takes off over the rooftops, in an attempt to escape the Fist of Khonshu's wrath.

It's time for a pursuit minigame!

Round one: Roll one die and add your **MIND**.

On a 6 or more: Take **+2** next round.

Get 5 or less: Take -1 next round.

Round two: Roll one die, and add your **MIND**, plus last round's adjustment. What's the result?

6 or more: turn to **292**.

5 or less: turn to **256**.

140

You realize that Moon Knight is not the only costumed super hero facing down the deathless horde swarming Times Square, when a figure drops from the top of a neon-lit billboard into the midst of the zombies and starts sending them flying, as they battle to protect the innocent and stop the horrors infecting anyone else with their undead contagion.

However, it is quite clear that the cursed canopic jar of the Pharaoh Akharis that is still gripped in the Mummy's bandaged hands is the source of the zombie plague. If Moon Knight can wrest it from N'Kantu and perhaps destroy it, then you hope that the effects of the spell can be reversed.

And so, Moon Knight prepares to battle his way through the ever-growing zombie horde to reach N'Kantu.

This is a moderately tough fight!

Round one: roll two dice and add your **MIGHT**. If you have an **[Ankh]** in your Inventory, add 1, but if you have a **[Khopesh]**, add 2. If the total is 12 or more, you win the first round.

Round two: roll two dice and add your **MIGHT**. If you have an [Ankh] in your Inventory, add 1, but if you have a [Khopesh], add 2, and if you won round one, add 1. If the total is 13 or more, you win the second round.

If you won the second round, turn to **90**.

If you lost the second round, turn to **120**.

141

Moon Knight sprints over to the nearest manhole cover and heaves it aside. When he suggested you go underground, you thought he meant you were going to take the subway.

"Hurry!" he calls, but with a zombie horde bearing down on you, you don't need any encouragement. No matter how unappealing entering the city's sewers, or wherever the manhole leads to, might be any other day of the week, right now you would rather wade through a river of stinking who-knows-what than succumb to the zombie plague.

As soon as you are through the hole, Moon Knight slides the iron cover back into place, leaving you hoping that none of the zombies has the sense to open it themselves.

Iron rungs hammered into a brick-lined shaft take you down to a maintenance tunnel lit by caged lamps that give off a dim yellow glow.

"We have to move fast," your companion instructs. "We don't want to upset the residents of Monster Metropolis."

"Monster what now?" you splutter. Has coming down here to escape the zombies been a classic case of frying pan and fire?

"A city located deep beneath the streets of Manhattan that is home to a myriad of creatures that most people don't believe even exist."

"There are mythological monsters living under New York?"

"Yes, so we don't want to hang around too long down here. Come on!"

From the maintenance tunnel you pass through a wheel-locked steel door into a ventilation shaft, over a rattling scaffold and down a rusted staircase to a concrete antechamber, and then through a hatch into a moldering brick-lined tunnel that reeks of effluent. A grilled walkway is bolted to one side with a sluggish current of foul-smelling water running alongside it.

You physically recoil at the stench and must fight to stop your gorge from rising.

Make an awareness test. Roll one die and add your **MIND** to it. What's the result?

>8 or more: turn to **18**.
>7 or less: turn to **4**.

142

"I was compelled to, just as I am compelled to become a savage beast every full moon," explains the Werewolf. "There is evil afoot here and we must sniff it out before its malign influence can spread any further."

Turn to **162**.

143

Taking Kraven the Hunter's **[Whip]** in hand, you crack it a few times to get the measure of it, then try to lash the Serpent with it. But rather than harming the monster, it only seems to make it mad. Take **-1 {SNAKEBITE}**.

There's no time to try anything else, as the enraged serpent strikes!

Turn to **192**.

144

All too painfully aware that time is fast running out, Moon Knight activates the [Tactical Grenade] and, in desperation, hurls it at the door of the Victorian house.

The device explodes, sending pink and purple shockwaves rippling across the surface of the magical shield. But when the smoke clears, the door to the building remains intact. It doesn't have so much as a scratch on it. Strike the [Tactical Grenade] from your Inventory.

Take +2 {NOISY NEIGHBOURS} and turn to 282.

145

"I do not care," the hunter spits back. "I have my prey in my sights already."

With that, he attacks your companion. This is going to be a tough fight.

Round one: roll two dice and add your MIGHT. If the total is 12 or more, you win the first round.

Round two: roll two dice and add your MIGHT. If you won the first round, add 1. If the total is 11 or more, you win the second round.

If you won the second round, turn to 108.

If you lost the second round, turn to 89.

146

Moon Knight rises to his feet, suddenly calm. Eerily so, in fact.

Why do you delay, my son? Khonshu demands of his avatar. *Do it now. Make the sacrifice!*

"You say the blood of the high priest is required to stop the ritual, but you haven't specified how much blood."

Moon Knight doesn't seem quite himself, in manner or tone. "Do you trust me?" he suddenly asks you, reaching for your wrist.

"Marc, are you all right?" you ask.

"Oh, I'm fine," he replies, "all things considered. But I'm not Marc, I'm Stephen. Stephen Grant. A pleasure to meet you at last."

What is going on? What has happened to Marc? And who is Stephen Grant?

> If you want to snatch your hand out of the way, turn to **122**.

> If you want to let Moon Knight take your hand and see what he does, turn to **134**.

147

Leaping into action, Moon Knight sprints after the fleeing Mummy. But as he does so, the jackals launch themselves at him, determined not to let him escape. Take **+1 {ECLIPSED}**.

This is a fight!

Round one: roll two dice and add your **MIGHT**. If the total is 11 or more, you win the first round.

Round two: roll two dice and add your **MIGHT**. If the total is 10 or more, you win the first round.

If you won both rounds, turn to **112**.

If you lost at least one of the rounds, turn to **131**.

148

Anubis's guard dogs defeated, Moon Knight turns to you and says, "Do you trust me? Let's find out."

Before you can answer, he grabs your wrist and draws the razor-sharp edge of a crescent-shaped dart across the palm of your open hand. You cry out as much in surprise as in pain, but the vigilante immediately releases his hold on you and flicks the blood that has collected on the blade into the air.

Turn to **82**.

149

Suddenly Moon Knight is there beside you, looking resplendent in his Kevlar bodyglove and crescent-shaped cloak, and with seemingly not a mark on him.

"You're back!" you exclaim in surprise.

"I never went away," Moon Knight replies.

ACHIEVEMENT: *Resurrection*.

With that, he launches an attack on the colossus, assaulting it with a barrage of crescents before leaping into the air and planting both feet against the giant's torso, sending it reeling. Before your eyes, the statue turns to sand and becomes one with the black dunes, as does the ruined temple complex behind it.

But that's not all that has changed. The moon is gone again from the sky – replaced instead by inverted mountains that drift by above you, seemingly so close you feel that you could almost reach out and touch them.

"Show yourself, demon!" Moon Knight shouts into the void.

The desert suddenly rises up before you as a tidal wave of sand. Within the sand forms a hideous face possessed of a demonic leer. Its mouth yawns open wide, and you are sure that it will swallow you any second. But worse than that are the thousands of iridescent purple-black scarab beetles that are pouring out of its eye sockets.

Make a terror test. Roll one die and add your {FEARFUL}. What's the result?

9 or more: turn to **169**.

8 or less: turn to **219**.

150

It doesn't matter how fast you run, or how skillfully Moon Knight dodges falling rocks or leaps over fallen columns, in the end you can't outrun the tectonic forces that have been unleashed by the interruption of the soul-stealing ritual.

With the patch of sunlight that demarcates the entrance to the tomb in sight, the roof of the hypostyle hall gives way and comes crashing down on top of you, burying you under a million tons of rock, more surely than the priests managed to hide King Tutankhamun's resting place. The difference is, no one will ever excavate your desert tomb.

ACHIEVEMENT: *Dead and Buried.*

Final score: 1 star.

The End.

151

"I won't let you face them alone!" Moon Knight tells his friend, as he leads the charge to meet the lumbering zombies, Frenchie's cries that he should make for the tomb going unheeded. Take **+1 {UNLOCKED}**.

There are not as many zombies here as you had to contend with in New York – the archaeological investigation team number only thirty souls – but they will still present Moon Knight with a challenging fight, even with Frenchie there to help him.

Round one: roll two dice and add your **MIGHT** and your

{UNLOCKED}. If the total is 18 or more, you win the first round.

Round two: roll two dice and add your **MIGHT** and, if you have any, your {ECLIPSED}. If the total is 19 or more, you win the second round.

Round three: roll two dice and add your **MIGHT** and, if you have any, your {UNLOCKED} and your {ECLIPSED}. If the total is 20 or more, you win the third round.

Subtract 1 from the number of rounds you won and adjust your **MIGHT** by that much: this could range from **+2** if you won all three, to **-1** if you lost all three.

If you won at least two rounds, turn to **97**.

If you lost two or more rounds, turn to **135**.

152

You suddenly become aware of other costumed super-powered individuals in Times Square as dozens of the newly created zombies are sent flying by their determined attacks. Moon Knight is not the only one who has been perturbed by N'Kantu's actions this night.

Take **+1 MYSTIC** and the ACHIEVEMENT: *Night of the Hunter.*

Leaving the others to deal with the ever-growing zombie horde, your companion makes for the mastermind behind this mess, N'Kantu the Living Mummy, while you do your best to keep up.

Turn to **90**.

153

Taking Kraven the Hunter's [Whip] from you, Moon Knight lashes it at the canopic jar held fast in N'Kantu's hands. The leather thong wraps around it and Moon Knight pulls, hoping to wrest the artifact from the Mummy's grip. But instead, the leather bursts into flames where it made contact with the blazing hieroglyphs, rendering the [Whip] useless.

Remove the [Whip] from your Inventory and take the ACHIEVEMENT: *Okey-dokey, Dr Jones*.

Roll one die. What is the result?

    1-3: turn to **209**.

    4-6: turn to **252**.

154

"We need to get to Times Square as quickly as possible," you remind the Fist of Khonshu.

    If you have an {UNLOCKED} of 1 or more, turn to **8**.

    If not, turn to **203**.

155

"Great Khonshu!" Moon Knight calls out, focusing his attention on the glowing orb that hangs over the city like a lantern, but which is currently smothered by clouds. "If I am your son, hear me now. Your avatar needs your aid!"

At precisely that moment, the clouds pass from before the face of the moon, and it is as if a beam of moonlight strikes the Grey Gargoyle full in the face. The villain throws up a hand to shield his eyes from its sudden unnatural brightness.

Seizing the opportunity, Moon Knight strikes, delivering a powerful kick to Grey Gargoyle's stomach that sends his enemy flying over the edge of the parapet and tumbling toward street level.

"Thank you, mighty Khonshu," your companion mutters under his breath and then turns to you. "We must refocus and stop N'Kantu before it is too late."

Take +1 {ECLIPSED}.

Turn to **106**.

156

Before Moon Knight can stop him, Black Spectre presses the button, and the bomb is triggered. The resulting explosion takes out a half-dozen parked cars and sends Mr Knight straight through a plate glass window.

As Detective Flint and the other police officers rush to secure the scene, you follow after, ignored by all of them. You reach the building, which has had its facade devastated by the explosion, as Mr Knight staggers out of the burning shop front, his clothes shredded by flying glass and soaked in his own blood.

"Time for a change of clothes, I think," Mr Knight says calmly as he walks back along Fifth Avenue to where his limousine stands waiting.

The cops watch him go, but nobody moves to stop him. They're clearly all too terrified.

Take +1 {FEARED} and -1 MIGHT and -1 MIND.

Turn to **206**.

157

Depressing the button on the [Tactical Grenade], you hurl it at the monster that now fills the chamber. You cannot miss, the grenade landing amidst the serpent's writhing coils, and a split second later, it detonates.

The concussive boom is deafening within the confines of the pyramidal space and leaves a painful ringing in your ears. But it has had the desired effect.

The ophidian monster writhes in agony and moment-arily recoils, allowing you to try something else, if you are able.

Take +2 {SNAKEBITE} and make a note that you cannot return to this section again.

Do you have anything else you think you could use against the serpent god?

If you do, turn back to **82** and try something you haven't tried previously.

If not, it's time to fight: turn to **192**.

158

The two of you set off through the city streets at a run, trying to stay ahead of the rapidly worsening outbreak. Following Seventh Avenue south, it doesn't take long for you to realize you are heading in the direction of Greenwich Village, and you point this out to Moon Knight.

"Of course!" he exclaims in something approaching delight. "There is one person in New York who is better prepared than anyone else to help us halt the spread of this zombie plague – and he has his base of operations in Greenwich Village."

An explosion suddenly rocks the street and a sheet of flame shoots across the highway, taking you both by surprise and causing you to come to an abrupt halt.

As your eyes adjust to the brightness of the flare you make out a female figure, silhouetted against the roaring flames that are consuming a taxi cab. Is she hurt? Was she caught in the blast?

As you instinctively move to help the woman, Moon Knight raises a hand and says, "Take care, my friend. I advise caution."

If you want to pause and wait to see what happens, turn to **102**.

If you want to ignore Moon Knight's warning and approach the figure, turn to **123**.

159

Moon Knight and N'Kantu the Living Mummy trade blows, the undead horror blocking the hero's karate kicks with his sinewy arms. At the same time, the

Mummy tries to lay his hands on Moon Knight so that he can either swing him against one of the stone statues or throttle the life out of him.

The Living Mummy staggers backward under a series of blows and for a moment it looks like Moon Knight is going to win the battle, but it turns out to be a ruse. The Mummy's retreat causes Moon Knight to overextend himself and it is then that N'Kantu fights back. Seizing the hero with both hands, the Mummy raises him above his head and hurls him at a slab of carved sandstone. The stone cracks in half at the impact and Moon Knight drops to the ground, winded. Take -1 MIGHT.

But rather than finish him off, the Mummy retrieves something from one of the displays of ancient Egyptian artifacts and flees before Moon Knight can give chase.

Turn to **105**.

160

"The sacrifice must be made," Moon Knight replies. "There is no other way."

Take -1 MIGHT and -1 MYSTIC.

With that, he leaps at you and, as you raise your hands to protect yourself, slashes the dart's razor edge across your outstretched palms.

Turn to **82**.

"Are you sure you're up to this?" Moon Knight challenges.

"When the moon god said we should stick together, I'm sure he only meant it metaphorically," you point out, more defensively than you might have intended.

"Very well," Moon Knight agrees, clearly not needing much persuading. It's bound to be easier for him to do what he's about to do without having to worry about you hanging around, quite literally.

"I'll stay here… and keep watch," you say helpfully.

Moon Knight fires his grapple and seconds later shoots up to the cathedral roof. Meanwhile, you try to look nonchalant, like you're used to lurking around street corners next to sleek, very expensive-looking limousines.

Several minutes go by, without anyone passing you on the street. You are just checking your watch for the umpteenth time when something dark and muscular drops from one of the ornate architectural features of the cathedral and lands on the sidewalk a few yards away. And it isn't Moon Knight.

Other than the gloves and boots he is wearing, which are blue, the man is gray from head to toe. In fact, he looks like a stone carving come to life.

"So, you are the Moon Knight's pet," he says in a thick French accent. "The Grey Gargoyle will deal with you like he dealt with your master!"

If you want to turn and run from the Grey Gargoyle, turn to **81**.

If you have something you think you could use to defend yourself, turn to **51**.

162

"Then it would appear that our purposes align," Moon Knight says. "N'Kantu must be stopped, and the artifact he stole from the museum recovered."

"You two should team up," you suggest. "Like Hawkeye and Lucky the Pizza Dog."

Moon Knight turns his cold stare upon you while a guttural growl rises from deep within the Werewolf's broad chest.

"I am nobody's pet to be kept restrained on a leash!" the lycanthrope bites back.

"No," agrees Moon Knight, "but there may be some sense in partnership. Then again, if we split up, we might have a greater chance of finding N'Kantu more quickly."

What's it to be? Should Moon Knight and the Werewolf:
Hunt for the Living Mummy together? Turn to **197**.
Search for N'Kantu separately? Turn to **178**.

163

Unfortunately, the dog whisperer act doesn't work. The growling gives way to full-on barking, then the jackals attack the pair of you together.

This is a fight!

Round one: roll two dice and add your **MIGHT**. If you have an **[Ankh]** in your Inventory, add 1, but if you have a **[Khopesh]**, add 2 instead. If the total is 11 or more, you win the first round.

Round two: roll two dice and add your **MIGHT**. If you have an **[Ankh]** in your Inventory, add 1, but if you have a **[Khopesh]**, add 2 instead. If the total is 10 or more, you win the second round.

If you won both rounds, turn to **112**.

If you lost at least one of the rounds, turn to **131**.

164

Having spent so many years studying the ancient Egyptians, something was strangely familiar about the incantation you heard N'Kantu chant as he enacted his dark rite to turn the population of New York into a zombie army.

Calling to mind those words now, you do your best to recite something akin to the spell the Living Mummy intoned. As you do so, the esoteric wards surrounding the Sanctum Sanctorum flare with a bright yellow light.

Take +1 {DARK POWER} and +1 {ABRACADABRA}.

Turn to **234**.

165

Finding your courage, you say, "Moon Knight is right. There is another far more dangerous son of Egypt loose in the city. You should be hunting him!"

Have you said enough to capture the hunter's attention?

Make a persuasion test. Roll one die and add your **MYSTIC** to it.

7 or more: turn to **127**.

6 or less: turn to **145**.

166

Activating the device, Moon Knight hurls the grenade into the heart of the howling vortex. Neither of you have any idea how long a fuse it has, and it explodes a second later with an earache-inducing bang. The bright flare the explosion produces blinds you temporarily. But was N'Kantu within the blast zone when it detonated?

Your vision returns as you blink the after-images of the explosion away and the smoke produced by the explosion clears.

Remove the [Tactical Grenade] from your Inventory and take the ACHIEVEMENT: *Son et Lumiere*.

Roll one die. What is the result?

    1-3: turn to **252**.

    4-6: turn to **194**.

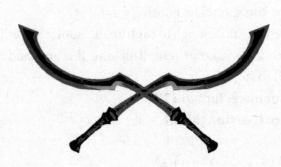

167

You have the eerie feeling that someone is watching you. You can feel gooseflesh rising on your arms and the hairs on the back of your neck stand on end. Looking up, you see that you are standing at the foot of a statue of Khonshu.

It is almost time, high priest, the moon god's voice echoes in your mind.

Take **+1 MIGHT**, **+1 MIND**, and **+1 MYSTIC**.

Turn to **187**.

168

It is quite clear that the cursed canopic jar of Akharis that is still gripped in the Mummy's bandaged hands is the source of the zombie plague. You hope that if Moon Knight can wrest if from N'Kantu, and perhaps destroy it, then the effects of the spell can be reversed. And so, Moon Knight battles his way through the massing zombie horde in order to reach N'Kantu.

This is a Moon Knight minigame!

Roll two dice and add your **MIGHT**, **MIND** and **MYSTIC**. Then add any {UNLOCKED}, {GRANTED}, {ECLIPSED}, {KNIGHTED} and {FEARED} you might have. If you have an [Ankh] in your Inventory, add 1, but if you have a [Khopesh], add 2. What is the final total?

20 or more: turn to **90**.

19 or less: turn to **120**.

169

You are utterly terrified, and you can feel your mind unraveling as you are bombarded by the nightmarish visions.

Take **-1 MIGHT**, **-2 MYSTIC**, and **-3 MIND**.

Stand strong in the face of adversity – it is the voice of Khonshu, carried on the desert wind – *and you shall prevail, priest.*

Make a sanity test. Roll two dice, add your **MIND** but deduct any {FEARFUL} or {AWED} you may have. What's the result?

9 or more: turn to **219**.

8 or less: turn to **189**.

170

"You're probably right," the Fist of Khonshu says. "We're more likely to spot N'Kantu at ground level, as he certainly won't be going high."

If it was some kind of test, you get the feeling that you passed.

The vigilante sets off down the steps of the museum, with you running to keep up. But, despite your breathlessness, you can't help vocalizing what you're thinking. "You're going to head to Times Square dressed like that? You'll either cause a panic or draw unwanted attention to yourself."

"Good point," Moon Knight agrees. "Wait here. I'll pick you up in a minute."

With that, the super hero deploys a grappling hook and sails away into the sky, disappearing behind an apartment building. As he does so, you are sure you hear him say, "Driver: go to the corner of 82nd and Madison. Town speed. Park."

Meanwhile, you are left alone on the sidewalk, looking lost. But only a matter of minutes later a white stretch limousine pulls up beside you. A door opens and you see a figure sitting inside, wearing a smart white suit, shirt, and tie. Even his shoes are white, as is the cloth hood that covers the entirety of his head.

"Get in," the man says.

"Moon Kn– ?" you begin before the limousine's passenger cuts you off.

"Call me *Mister* Knight."

You do as you are bidden and make yourself comfortable within the plush interior of the limousine. But what's with this Mr Knight persona? Take **+1 {KNIGHTED}**.

"Driver: Times Square. Town speed."

You're not sure who's driving the car, but they pull out into the traffic and set off along Fifth Avenue. However, it's not long before the limousine comes to a virtual stop again.

"Driver: what seems to be the problem?"

"*Roadblock ahead,*" comes an emotionless electronic voice from speakers in the back of the limo. "*Diversion in operation.*"

You wonder out loud what's going on.

"Whatever it is, we don't have time for it," mutters Mr Knight in annoyance.

"But if the road's closed, surely the best thing we can do is go with the flow," you say.

"Perhaps. Or I could investigate."

> If you think Mr Knight should get out and investigate, turn to **16**.
>
> If you think you should both remain in the limousine and let the driver follow the diversion, turn to **64**.

171

Thirty minutes later, you arrive. The Akh'ran Highlands rise from the surrounding wilderness, creating a tangle of desolate ochre peaks and deeply shaded gorges, and at their heart lies the temporary settlement occupied by the archeological expedition. Despite the presence of the shanty town of tents that has sprung up here, the place appears to be deserted; tools lie discarded in the dust, vehicles abandoned, and the excavations remain unattended.

"I thought you said the site was overrun with zombies," Moon Knight says as the three of you disembark from the helicopter.

"And it was," Frenchie replies, sounding hurt that his old friend would doubt him. "Where is everyone?"

Duchamp has brought you to one end of a steep-sided, dead-end valley among the mountainous hills. Great cliff walls surround you on three sides. At the end of the valley, in the shadows that have collected there, you can see the opening to the complex the archaeologists have been investigating. At the opposite end of the valley is the temporary encampment of canvas structures and prefabricated shelters. This is where the team has been living while they work on the site, and where they have been recording their finds.

"Let's take a look around," suggests Moon Knight. As he makes for the opening at the end of the valley, Frenchie heads toward the spot where the team's all-terrain vehicles are parked, while you make for the nearest tent.

Pulling back the canvas flap that is the entrance to one of the marquees, you expect to see tables laid with various finds, but instead the first thing your eyes land on is a wooden crate filled with straw, within which are packed several [Sticks of Dynamite].

A cry from Frenchie alerts you and Moon Knight to the fact that the archaeologists have revealed themselves at last. They are coming from the direction of the tented village at the other end of the valley.

"Hurry!" shouts Frenchie. "Into the temple!" He takes a pistol from a holster at his belt. "Go! I will keep them at bay," he declares, racking the slide and chambering a round.

Which of the following Qualities has the highest score at present?

{UNLOCKED}: turn to **151**.

{GRANTED}: turn to **97**.

{ECLIPSED}: turn to **115**.

If they are all equal, turn to **228**.

172

Now is the time, my son, you hear the booming voice of Khonshu echoing inside your skull once more. *Make the sacrifice!*

"No!" he roars. "There has to be another way!"

But before Moon Knight has time to consider an alternative method to disrupt the ritual, with barely a word from Anubis, the jackals launch themselves at your companion.

Moon Knight will have to deal with the jackals quickly.

Round one: roll two dice and add your **MIGHT**, along with your {UNLOCKED}. If the total is 14 or more, you win the first round.

Round two: roll two dice and add your **MIGHT**, along with your {UNLOCKED}. If the total is 15 or more, you win the second round.

If you won the second round, turn to **148**.

If you lost the second round, turn to **214**.

173

Scanning the floor tiles, you identify a pattern in the hieroglyphs. The slabs have not been placed randomly. In fact, the order in which they have been laid is of vital significance.

And so, you guide Moon Knight as he sets off across the room, taking care to only step on one floor tile at a time, sticking to only those that are found in the royal name of King Akharis, until your companion finally reaches the other side. Once he is safely across, you follow, taking exactly the same route, and join him at the entrance to another passageway.

Turn to **264**.

174

Unsurprisingly, Moon Knight is exhausted by his battle with the monstrous serpent. Despite putting up a valiant defense, in the end the creature's speed, savage fangs, and colossal size get the better of the super hero. As the Fist of Khonshu stumbles, you watch in horror as the Serpent God seizes his chance. Jaws wide, the giant snake catches Moon Knight in its mouth and swallows the vigilante whole.

Then it turns its mesmerizing ophidian gaze on you...
The End.

175

Taking out the vial of Duval's serum, you throw it at the serpent. The glass shatters on contact with the monster's bone-hard scales, bathing its writhing coils in the petrifying agent. However, it soon becomes clear that Seth's inhuman physiology is not affected by the serum.

If you act quickly, there may still be time to try something else.

If you have something else you want to try, turn back to **82** and choose an option you haven't tried before. If not, turn to **192**.

176

While Moon Knight might be the avatar of Khonshu, and therefore imbued with a portion of his god's power, Shadow Knight himself has undergone a series of "lunar treatments," which have granted him superhuman strength and durability.

Moon Knight lashes out with a powerful roundhouse kick, but his dark mirror image deflects it with one arm, while delivering a vicious punch with the other. He follows this up with a chest kick of his own that sends the vigilante flying across the roof. Moon Knight lands in a breathless heap against the supports of the water tank.

"Sweet dreams, brother!" Shadow Knight laughs cruelly, and then he is gone into the night, swallowed by the shadows that cluster about the surrounding tenement buildings.

Take **-1 MIGHT** and **+2 {SWEET DREAMS}**.

You go to help Moon Knight, but he has already shaken off the head-reeling effects of his brother's assault. "Randall will have to wait, for now. We still need to catch up with N'Kantu."

Turn to **106**.

177

"Dark magic is at work here," states Moon Knight grimly, "so what we need is aid of a magical nature, and there is no one better qualified to provide it in all the city – in fact, anywhere on Earth – than Doctor Strange, Master of the Mystic Arts and the Sorcerer Supreme."

Take **+1 MIGHT**, **+1 MIND**, and **+1 MYSTIC**, along with the ACHIEVEMENT: *Secret Three*.

Now turn to **267**.

178

"Agreed," says the Werewolf.

With that, he takes off along the alleyway, running on all fours, and vanishes around a corner. You and Moon Knight set off again at a run, headed for Times Square.

Take **+1 {HUNTED}** and the ACHIEVEMENT: *Off the Leash*.

Now turn to **280**.

179

Snapping out of his stupor, Moon Knight springs at the undead horror. But N'Kantu the Living Mummy was once a mighty warrior himself. He led a bloody uprising against the pharaoh who had enslaved his tribe, and knows one or two tricks himself, and so will not be easily thwarted.

This is a fight!

Round one: roll two dice and add your **MIGHT**. If the total is 10 or more, you win the first round.

Round two: roll two dice and add your **MIGHT**. If you won the first round, add 1. If your total is 9 or more, you win the second round.

If you won the second round, turn to **129**.

If you lost the second round, turn to **159**.

180

"Khonshu, aid me now," Moon Knight cries, as he launches himself at the Living Mummy. "Let your Fist deliver your vengeance!"

Make a chutzpah test. Roll one die, and add your **MYSTIC** to it, but deduct your {**AWED**}, if you have any. What's the result?

8 or more: turn to **194**.

7 or less: turn to **209**.

181

"I wish I could say all the better for seeing you, Randall," says Moon Knight, "but we both know that would be a lie. This individual is my younger brother," he adds by way of introduction. "You can probably see the family resemblance."

"I prefer to go by Shadow Knight," counters the other. "Perhaps it's time we settled our little family feud once and for all."

What does Moon Knight say in reply?

"Then let's finish it, here and now!" Turn to **243**.

"Brother, there are more important things to focus on tonight than our strained familial relationship." Turn to **9**.

"We are both members of the Cult of Khonshu, and our god has need of us this night." Turn to **276**.

182

"Have at you, foul keepers of the graveyard," Moon Knight snarls as he arms himself with a pair of deadly razor edged crescent-shaped throwing weapons. Take **+1 {UNLOCKED}**.

With that, the jackals attack you both. This is a fight!

Round one: roll two dice and add your **MIGHT**. If you have an **[Ankh]** in your Inventory, add 1, but if you have a **[Khopesh]**, add 2. If the total is 11 or more, you win the first round.

Round two: roll two dice and add your **MIGHT**. If you have an [Ankh] in your Inventory, add 1, but if you have a [Khopesh], add 2. If the total is 10 or more, you win the second round.

If you won both rounds, turn to **112**.

If you lost at least one of the rounds, turn to **131**.

183

"The sacrifice must be made in the name of Khonshu, protector of all those who travel by night, whose vengeance knows no bounds," Moon Knight says in an emotionless monotone.

He draws one of his razor-sharp crescents, ready to strike you down, you are sure.

"Marc, wait!" you cry out in desperation. "Don't do this! I'm your friend. This isn't you. This is Khonshu's will, not yours! There has to be another way."

Moon Knight hesitates, his arm frozen, and you believe you see his features twisting beneath the white cloth mask, as if he is enduring some inner turmoil.

Make a willpower test. Roll one die and add your **MYSTIC** and **MIND** to it, but deduct any {DARK POWER} you may have. What's the result?

Total of 10 or more: turn to **172**.

9 or less: turn to **160**.

184

Speaking into his communicator, Moon Knight summons a swarm of drones, each no bigger than a briefcase. You anxiously watch the approaches that lead to the Sanctum Sanctorum as the ever-growing horde that is advancing from every direction closes on your position, praying that the drones arrive before the zombies reach you.

And then, suddenly, a score of self-propelled robotic drones come in over the rooftops and launch a fusillade of energy pulses at the brownstone. Light ripples across the warding shield with every impact, but not one of them penetrates the magical barrier.

Take **+3 {NOISY NEIGHBOURS}** and turn to **282**.

185

Black Spectre might be down, but Mr Knight isn't finished with him yet. The villain suffers a savage beating that leaves him in a bloodied heap on the ground, gasping for breath, and with blood pouring from his broken nose and mouth.

Judging by the reactions of Detective Flint and the other cops watching events unfold from the sidelines, the vigilante has crossed a line and not done himself any favors in the eyes of the NYPD. You're not so sure you want to spend any more time in his company either, but it doesn't look like you have a choice in the matter.

Take **+1 {FEARED}** then turn to **206**.

186

Fast as a pair of striking cobras, the two hunters engage in battle. As they trade blows, it is clear that Kraven is dangerously adept at using his whip, while Moon Knight is just as dangerous as he lays about him with his baton. Take **+1 {UNLOCKED}**.

This is a fight!

Round one: roll two dice and add your **MIGHT**. If the total is 12 or more, you win the first round.

Round two: roll two dice and add your **MIGHT**. If you won the first round, add 1. If the total is 11 or more, you win the second round.

If you won the second round, turn to **108**.

If you lost the second round, turn to **89**.

187

Reaching the end of the gallery, you and Moon Knight flatten yourselves against the wall, and peer around the edge of the gate into the space beyond.

You are looking into a large space shaped like the inside of a hollow pyramid, its four walls converging at a point high above the chamber floor. The inconstant, multi-colored luminescence forces you to squint, so you cannot make out anything else about the chamber, such as what it contains, and the lightshow is accompanied by a rushing sound as if a gale is blowing within the shrine.

It is because of these distractions that you do not realize you are in danger until the zombie is upon you.

Moon Knight spins around as the thing lays a clawing hand on his cloak and immediately gives voice to a gasp of horror. It is not just any zombie, it is Jean-Paul "Frenchie" Duchamp, and the Fist of Khonshu has no choice but to defend himself.

This is a fight!

Round one: roll two dice and add your **MIGHT**. If the total is 14 or more, you win the first round.

Round two: roll two dice and add your **MIGHT**. If you won the first round, add 1. If your total is 15 or more, you win the second round.

> If you won the second round, Moon Knight ties Frenchie up using one of his own bootlaces, so he cannot do anyone any more harm: turn to **289**.

If you lost the second round, turn to **207**.

188

"I was hoping you might be able to tell us that," Moon Knight replies.

"Why?" asks the Frenchman, with a shrug.

"Because you're my man on the ground."

"But at present we are in the air," Duchamp points out.

"Do you not have any ideas?" Moon Knight challenges him.

"Well, you say you are looking for a temple. The site I was helping to protect has the features of a temple complex but dug into the mountains. We could start there. But I doubt there's anyone left at the dig site who hasn't succumbed to the zombie plague," Frenchie says, his voice solemn.

Take **-1 MIND** and **-1 MYSTIC**.

Turn to **171**.

189

Everything that has befallen you and Moon Knight since N'Kantu stole the cursed canopic jar from the Metropolitan Museum of Art has turned your world upside down and taken its toll on your sanity. Not only that, but it has hammered away at the vigilante's damaged psyche as well. You can take it no longer. Your reason crumbles under the onslaught of living nightmares that assail your mind, and you become irrevocably insane. There is no way back from this. You will remain trapped in the Dream Dimension for all eternity, forced to suffer the same unending mental torment again and again and again.

The End.

190

"Or we could take to the sky, in one of your drones," you suggest, adding a third option to the list.

Moon Knight nods his head slowly. "That's a good idea, actually. We could, but would we be any wiser as to where N'Kantu has gone? If it's where I think it is, the Moon-Wing doesn't have a great enough range to get there. So many choices seem like the right one, but how do we decide on the best course of action?"

How do you want to reply?

> "Surely, right now, we just need to worry about getting away from the zombies, so let's get airborne." Turn to **119**.
>
> "Very well, let's stick to the streets." Turn to **158**.
>
> "OK, let's go underground." Turn to **141**.

191

Moon Knight pilots the drone over the labyrinthine network of streets beneath, heading south toward Times Square, on the lookout for N'Kantu the Living Mummy. However, as you pass over the southernmost limits of Central Park and on over Midtown you hear a rushing sound and a moment later the drone is sent into a spin as something hits the starboard wing and explodes.

A cacophony of hazard sirens starts to sound from the drone's beleaguered systems, and you hear Moon Knight call out, "Hold tight and brace for impact! We're going down!"

You only took off a minute or so ago, but now your very life depends upon how well Moon Knight can keep control of the drone's controls as the craft plummets out of the sky, its starboard wing shredded by the rocket that hit it.

Make an emergency landing test. Roll one die and add your MIGHT and MIND to it. What's the result?

Total of 10 or more: turn to 77.

9 or less: turn to **49**.

192

Moon Knight has fought many epic battles against some of the most dangerous villains in the world – not to mention some of its greatest super heroes – but has there ever been a battle as epic as this?

This is an uber-boss level fight!

Before battle begins, if you have any {DARK POWER} deduct it from any {SNAKEBITE} you might have.

Round one: roll two dice and add your MIGHT and any {SNAKEBITE} you might have but deduct any {AWED}. If you have a [Khopesh] add 2. If the total is 23 or more, you win the first round.

Round two: roll two dice and add your MIGHT and MYSTIC and any {SNAKEBITE}. If you have an [Ankh] add 2. If the total is 24 or more, you win the second round.

Round three: roll two dice and add your MIGHT and MIND and any {SNAKEBITE}. If you have a [Khopesh] add 2, and/or if you have an [Ankh] add 1. If the total is 24 or more, you win the third round.

Round four: roll two dice and add your **MIND** and **MYSTIC** and any {SNAKEBITE}. If you have an [Eye of Horus] add 2. If the total is 25 or more, you win the fourth round.

Round five: roll two dice and add your **MIGHT**, **MIND** and **MYSTIC**, plus any {SNAKEBITE}. If you have a [Khopesh] add 1, if you have an [Ankh] add 1, and/or if you have an [Eye of Horus] add 2. If the total is 25 or more, you win the fifth round.

If you won three or more rounds, turn to **128**.

If you lost three or more rounds, turn to **174**.

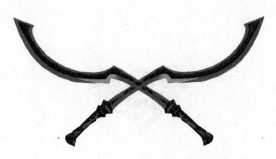

193

Moon Knight sets off across the chamber without a second thought. You are about to do the same when you hear a *pfft! pfft!* of air and a dozen darts fly out of holes in the adjacent walls, with Moon Knight being caught in the crossfire.

Several of the darts strike the super hero's cloak or armored bodyglove and do not penetrate his skin, but others make direct contact with his flesh.

Roll one die, add 6, and deduct that much **MIGHT**.

If your **MIGHT** is zero or below, turn immediately to **213**.

If not, it is only then that you identify a pattern in the arrangement of the floor tiles. Taking your life in your hands, you cross the chamber, fortunately without coming to any harm, and instruct Moon Knight to follow precisely in your footsteps,: turn to **264**.

194

With his enemy on the back foot, Moon Knight delivers a powerful punch to the Living Mummy that almost causes him to drop the cursed canopic jar. Placing it on a step before any harm can come to it, N'Kantu goes to grab Moon Knight by the neck, seeking to throttle the life from Khonshu's chosen avatar.

This is a boss fight!

Round one: roll two dice and add your **MIGHT** and, if you have any, your {UNLOCKED}. If the total is 13 or more, you win the first round.

Round two: roll two dice and add your **MIGHT** and, if you have any, your {GRANTED}. If you won round one, add 1. If the total is 14 or more, you win the second round.

Round three: roll two dice and add your **MIGHT** and, if you have any, your {ECLIPSED}. If you won round two, add 2. If the total is 15 or more, you win the third round.

Subtract 1 from the number of rounds you won and adjust your **MIGHT** by that much: this could range from **+2** if you won all three, to **-1** if you lost all three.

If you won at least two rounds, turn to **110**.

If you lost at least two rounds, turn to **125**.

195

You load a bolt into the flight groove of the crossbow and, your hands shaking, take aim. Fortunately, Khonshu, or some other higher power, is with you, and you score a direct hit. Take **+2** {SNAKEBITE}.

Your shot does not kill the serpent, but it does enrage it. There's no time to try anything else, as the monster attacks.

Turn to **192**.

The jackals are in motionless heaps on the floor. Moon Knight stands between them, panting for breath, the white armor of Khonshu covered with the blood of his enemies. Take **+1 MIGHT**.

Now is the time, my son, comes the booming voice of Khonshu again. *Make the sacrifice!*

With that, the instrument of the moon god's vengeance starts to stride toward you, his knuckles bunching beneath the studded cesti knuckle-duster gauntlets.

"Moon Knight, don't do this!" you cry out in desperation. "I'm your friend. After all that we have been through together since we met, Marc, you do not want to do this!"

"Not Marc," Moon Knight snarls, "Lockley!" But he halts his advance and puts his bunched fists to his head, as if wrestling with some inner turmoil.

Make a willpower test. Roll one die, and add your **MYSTIC** and **MIND** to it, but deduct any **{DARK POWER}** you have. What's the result?

Total of 10 or more: turn to **109**.

9 or less: turn to **86**.

197

Suddenly alert, the wolfman sniffs the air. "I've got his scent," he says. "It's like sand and formaldehyde."

"Then lead the way, Jack," Moon Knight says. Take **+1 {GOOD DOG}**.

The two of you follow as the shapeshifter bounds along the alleyway, before disappearing around a corner. You have to run to keep up, turning where the Werewolf turns, until he stops at the edge of Times Square.

There, standing at the top of the stepped platform that forms the roof of the TKTS discount ticket booth at the center of the Square is N'Kantu the Living Mummy.

The revelers who pack the square are so caught up with themselves, taking selfies and posing for videos, that they barely even register his presence. Either that or they think he's a pro-level cosplayer. Or maybe he is drawing on the dark power of the canopic jar to mask his presence here.

You can feel waves of malign energy emanating from the ancient artifact even at this distance. It makes your skin crawl and your neurons fizz, as if your very DNA is being rewritten the longer you are exposed to it.

Jack Russell bristles, his lupine senses on fire. "We have to stop him!" he growls. "And fast!"

"But N'Kantu doesn't know we are here," Moon Knight points out. "We have the element of surprise, which gives us the advantage. We should use stealth to make our approach."

"All the more reason why we should attack now!" the Werewolf barks.

Moon Knight turns to you to settle the matter. "What do you think?"

How do you want to answer?

"Attack now." Turn to **255**.

"Use stealth." Turn to **235**.

198

Pointing the ray gun-like device at the Victorian brownstone, you pull the trigger. A wave of thrumming sound is emitted by the weapon, which rattles the teeth in your head and causes the magical shield protecting the Sanctum Sanctorum to ripple in agitation. You keep your finger pressed against the trigger until the sonic disruptor's power cell is spent. Strike the [Alien Device] from your Inventory.

Despite the noise the device made, it has not had the desired effect and the building's occupier doesn't come to the door. However, as the echoes of the sonic assault reverberate along Bleecker Street, you hear the approaching zombie horde cry out in response. They are getting closer all the time.

Take +2 {NOISY NEIGHBOURS} and turn to **282**.

199

"You are pathetic, not worthy of the great Grey Gargoyle's attentions," the villain boasts, "but I shall put you out of your misery nonetheless."

Whatever you're going to do, you had better do it fast.

Make a quick-thinking test. Roll one die and add your MIND to it. What's the result?

Total of 6 or more: turn to **222**.

5 or less, you can't think your way out of your situation, so you will have to try something else. Take -1 MIND.

If you have a [Khopesh], and you want to use it now, turn to **35**.

If you have a golden [Ankh], and you want to use that, turn to **15**.

If you just want to run for it, turn to **81**.

200

Spurred on by Moon Knight's example, you follow the trail he blazes as he dodges falling statues and vaults over toppled columns. Eventually the patch of sunlight that demarcates the entrance to the tomb appears at the end of the hypostyle hall by which you entered.

Even as the pillars start to come apart and fall like papyrus stems before the reaper's scythe, you, Frenchie, and Moon Knight fling yourselves through the doorway and into scorching sunlight. The roof of the chamber collapses behind you in a roar of noise and dust.

Picking yourselves up out of the sand at the bottom of the temple steps, you are met by the stunned faces of the archaeological dig team. Mindless zombies no more, they stare at you dumbfounded, having no idea what you have done or what happened to them.

If you needed any further proof that your mission has been a success, this is it. And if the archaeologists and laborers have returned to normal, then surely so will everyone else who succumbed to the zombie plague.

As Moon Knight walks among them, they fall to their knees as if in worship, and you consider all that has happened since the two of you first met. But ultimately, you have defeated Seth, escaped death on numerous occasions, and saved the world. Why, anyone would think you were nearly a super hero yourself.

ACHIEVEMENT: *Super Hero Sidekick.*

Final score: 2 stars.

The End.

201

You pass Doctor Strange the artifact, and he hands you the ominous looking [Black Grimoire] in return.

"Be warned," the sorcerer says before releasing his hold on the book, "only use this in the direst of circumstances."

Take +1 {DARK POWER}.

A cataclysmic boom shakes the Sanctum Sanctorum, and Doctor Strange shoots you an anxious look.

Turn to **297**.

202

As Moon Knight continues to talk to them, the wild dogs' growling quietens until they are not growling at all. Their posture changes, too. Rather than prowling toward him, they trot over with tails wagging.

"Good dogs," he says, offering the jackals his hand to lick.

"I didn't know you were a dog person," you joke.

Moon Knight seems to smile, even behind his mask. "They only needed some gentle guidance."

"Much like wayward Egyptologists?" you mock.

"Oh no. Egyptologists are far more troublesome."

At least the jackals won't be troubling you now.

Leaving the zoo, the two of you follow a path that leads toward a line of trees. They have lost all definition in the darkness, while beneath them even darker shadows have gathered.

Turn to **204**.

203

"My conscience is quite correct," the sharp-suited crime fighter tells the detective. "If this were any other night I would help you, but not this night. I can't. I'm sorry."

With Detective Flint's protestations echoing in your ears, the two of you get back into the limousine and nudge your way back into the crawling traffic.

Take **+1 {FEARED}**.

Turn to **64**.

204

As you approach the trees, Moon Knight suddenly stops, putting out an arm that brings you to a halt, too. At that instant, a figure drops from a branch to land in front of you. It is a muscular, bearded man wearing a striking costume that makes it look like his head and torso are emerging from a roaring lion's face.

In his hand he holds a whip, which he cracks as he growls, "The Moon Knight. Are you a prey worthy of Sergei Kravinoff?"

"It is not me you should be hunting, Kraven," the Fist of Khonshu declares.

You are now facing the master tactician and tracker Kraven the Hunter, and it looks like he and your companion are squaring up for a fight.

If you want to stand back and let them get on with it, turn to **186**.

If you want to interrupt their posturing by asking for Kraven's help, turn to **165**.

205

"Down there!" you shout over the wind, and Moon Knight curses when he catches sight of the figure. Take **+1 MIND**.

As you watch, this knight of shadows takes off over the rooftops, in an attempt to escape the Fist of Khonshu.

It's time for a pursuit minigame!

Round one: Roll one die and add your **MIND**.

On a 6 or more: Take **+2** next round.

Get 5 or less: Take **-1** next round.

Round two: Roll one die, and add your **MIND**, plus last round's adjustment. What's the result?

6 or more: turn to **292**.

5 or less: turn to **256**.

206

"It's time we were gone," Mr Knight says, and despite everything you have witnessed – or perhaps precisely because of everything you have witnessed – you feel compelled to obey.

You are only a half-mile from Times Square, so your companion decides to abandon the limousine and his Mr Knight persona, and continue on foot.

Back in his Moon Knight body armor, the vigilante leads the way, keeping to secluded alleys and backstreets as much as possible. And then you see it, staggering along the alleyway ahead of you, its lumbering gait giving it away immediately. It is N'Kantu the Living Mummy!

"The moon be praised!" your companion hisses under his breath and springs forward.

In that instant, something drops from a fire escape above you and lands in a lupine crouch between you and Moon Knight, and the Mummy.

You cannot hide your shock and astonishment, and gasp in surprise. The creature is humanoid in form, but his muscular body is covered with a thick layer of fur. His teeth are long and pointed, as are his ears, and his fingernails have grown to become ragged claws. The only concession he has made to clothing is a pair of torn jeans, and they're not ripped in the fashionable way.

First a Mummy and now a Werewolf? You feel you have truly glimpsed beyond the veil this night.

The wolfman's eyes blaze the color of blood and a savage snarl escapes his throat. Meanwhile, N'Kantu is getting away.

> If you think Moon Knight should attack the Werewolf, turn to **226**.
>
> If you think Moon Knight should wait to see if the Werewolf makes the first move, turn to **246**.
>
> If you think the vigilante should ignore the creature and go after N'Kantu, turn to **268**.

207

Perhaps it is because he is being forced to fight his old and faithful friend that Moon Knight doesn't land his blows as hard as he could, or perhaps it is just that the last several hours have taken their toll on him and he is exhausted. Whatever the reason, the zombie resists Moon Knight's blows until Frenchie's innate cunning spots an opportunity and grabs it with both hands – or rather, his teeth.

With Moon Knight down, Frenchie turns his attention toward you. You back away, attempting to escape into the pyramidal chamber. You do not manage to get very far before the Fist of Khonshu rises again, no longer the protector of those who travel by night, but now one of those who would threaten their safety.

You have no hope against both of them and become the next victim of the zombie plague.

The End.

208

Your destination lies in the Al Shalateen Desert, Khonshu's voice booms in your ears, making you start.

Moon Knight repeats this information for Duchamp's benefit, the Frenchman clearly not having a psychic link to the God of the Moon.

"But that's where I've just come from!" he exclaims. "Specifically, the Highlands."

"Then you won't have any problems finding it," Moon Knight says.

Take **+1 MYSTIC** and the ACHIEVEMENT: *Divine Inspiration.*

Now turn to **171**.

209

Moon Knight goes to deliver a powerful punch to the Mummy's face, but N'Kantu manages to deflect it with an arm that is like iron since it was soaked in magical chemicals three thousand years ago. Placing the canopic jar on the floor, before any harm can befall it, his hands free now,

N'Kantu goes to grab Moon Knight by the neck so that he might throttle the life from Khonshu's chosen avatar.

This is a boss fight!

Round one: roll two dice and add your **MIGHT** and, if you have any, your {UNLOCKED}. If the total is 15 or more, you win the first round.

Round two: roll two dice and add your **MIGHT** and, if you have any, your {GRANTED}. If you won round one, add 1. If the total is 14 or more, you win the second round.

Round three: roll two dice and add your **MIGHT** and, if you have any, your {ECLIPSED}. If you won round two, add 2. If the total is 15 or more, you win the third round.

Subtract 1 from the number of rounds you won and adjust your **MIGHT** by that much: this could range from **+2** if you won all three, to **-1** if you lost all three.

If you won at least two rounds, turn to **110**.

If you lost at least two rounds, turn to **125**.

210

As soon as all of the stone keys are located in the correct slots, two things happen. First of all, the flow of sand filling the chamber comes to an abrupt stop. Secondly, with a grinding of stone, the block that dropped down over the chamber entrance begins to rise.

As soon as the space beneath it is large enough for Moon Knight to squeeze through, without a moment's hesitation he does just that, calling for you to follow him. Fearing that the stone might drop back down at any moment, you take your life in your hands and duck under it yourself.

Take the ACHIEVEMENT: *Codebreaker*.

Now turn to **98**.

211

The north side of Times Square is completely overrun with zombies and the plague appears to be spreading into the adjoining thoroughfares. The path with least resistance lies to the south.

Moon Knight turns his furious, white-eyed gaze upon you. "The way I see it, we can stick to the city streets, or we can head underground to avoid the zombie hordes."

If you think the pair of you should stick to the streets, turn to **158**.

If you think it would be better to head underground, turn to **141**.

And if you have a {KNIGHTED} of 2 or more, and you do not have a {CRASH LANDING} of 1, you could turn to **190** instead.

212

"There!" Moon Knight declares. "Khonshu shows us the way."

The moon hangs over the city. It could be your imagination, especially bearing in mind your heightened agitated state, but it seems like its cold, wan light is illuminating the Central Park Zoo.

"Hurry!" Moon Knight calls as he sets off down the museum steps, heading toward the park. "We will soon have our quarry within our grasp."

Take **+1 MYSTIC** and the ACHIEVEMENT: *Secret One*.

Now turn to **242**.

213

Moon Knight falls to the ground and doesn't get up again. In a panic, and not knowing what else to do, you run over to help him, hoping that all the darts were expended when he triggered the trap. Fortunately for you, they were.

Kneeling beside the super hero, you pull off his mask to reveal the face beneath. Moon Knight's eyes are tightly closed, and he is sweating profusely, while his skin is pale and his breathing is shallow. Whatever was on the tips of those darts, it is taking a terrible toll on his constitution. For all you know, he might even die!

But perhaps you have something in your Inventory that could help him?

If you have an [Ankh], turn to **251**.

If not, turn to **231**.

214

Moon Knight lies pinned to the sandy floor of the chamber by one of the monstrous jackals, while the other bounds toward you. You cannot avoid its tearing claws and snapping teeth, and as you try to fend it off, the cadaverous canine manages to bite your hand. Take **-1 MIGHT**.

As you pull it away abruptly, blood flies from the savage wound.

Turn to **82**.

215

"So does that mean you'll help?" Flint asks, but Mr Knight has vanished.

As you both scour the street, trying to work out where the crime fighter has gone, something swoops overhead – something clad in an armored bodyglove and riding the wind on a broad, crescent-shaped cloak.

Black Spectre has seen him too. As the villain raises his weapons to defend himself, Moon Knight sweeps down out of the night sky like a moon-launched missile.

Make an aerial maneuvers test. Roll two dice and add your **MIGHT** and **MIND**. What's the result?

13 or more: turn to **229**.

12 or less: turn to **249**.

216

Taking the device in hand, you point it at the serpent and pull the trigger. Rather than a beam of focused laser energy, a wave of concussive sound bursts from the weapon and strikes the horror. The monster recoils as it is bombarded by the soundwaves pulsing from the sonic disruptor.

You really couldn't have chosen a more effective weapon to use against the giant serpent, but as you keep your finger pressed against the trigger, the device soon drains its power cell, rendering it useless.

Take **+3 {SNAKEBITE}** and strike the [Alien Device] from your Inventory.

Do you have something else you could use against the serpent god?

If you do, turn back to **82** and try something you haven't used previously.

If not, it's time to fight: turn to **192**.

217

Grabbing the staff, you hold it out before you, hoping to keep the advancing Mummy beyond arm's reach. You doubt a glorified wooden stick will hold the undead horror at bay for long, but you certainly aren't expecting what happens next.

The rod in your hand abruptly transforms into a writhing serpent. The snake hisses and strikes the Mummy, sinking its fangs into the monster's alchemically preserved flesh. Your opponent snarls – either in pain or annoyance, or maybe both – and tears the snake from his arm before hurling it away into some dark corner.

An almighty crash from above has you both looking to the ceiling, and you fix your eyes on a shadowy figure that is descending amidst a shower of glass shards, a crescent-shaped cloak spread out behind it. Take +1 {ECLIPSED}.

The figure lands in a crouch between you, before rising to its full height of six feet and two inches. The man turns to you then and you see that his face is covered by a white mask. Your savior's bodyglove, cloak, and cowl are white as well, and seem to glow in the moonlight.

"Are you all right?" the figure asks.

But all you can say in reply is, "M-moon Knight?"

Turn to **88**.

218

You are out of time. The zombie hordes have caught up with you at last.

To stand against the horde seems like an impossible task. No matter how many you and Moon Knight manage to put out of action, like the heads of the hydra, when one falls there will be at least two more ready to take its place. And more are arriving from every corner of Greenwich Village all the time.

But something inside Moon Knight will not let him give in to the zombies and willingly become one of them. He is the Fist of Khonshu, and he clearly feels compelled to fight. As long as there is breath within his lungs, he will continue to mete out the moon god's divine vengeance until the bitter end.

This is a tough fight.

Round one: roll two dice and add your **MIGHT** and, if you have any, your {UNLOCKED}. If the total is 23 or more, you win the first round.

Round two: roll two dice and add your **MIGHT** and, if you have any, your {ECLIPSED}. If the total is 24 or more, you win the second round.

Round three: roll two dice and add your **MIGHT** and, if you have any, your {UNLOCKED} and your {ECLIPSED}. If the total is 25 or more, you win the third round.

Subtract 1 from the number of rounds you won and adjust your **MIGHT** by that much: this could range from **+2** if you won all three, to **-1** if you lost all three.

If you win the third round, turn to **234**.

If you lose the third round, turn to **107**.

219

You somehow manage to cling onto the last vestiges of your sanity and find the courage to stand firm in the face of the horrific visions and unsettling sensations that nonetheless feel all too real. Moon Knight stands at your side, lending you the courage you need to remain strong.

"I say again, demon, in the name of Khonshu the Mighty, reveal yourself!" Moon Knight bellows.

The face reverts to a towering wall of sand which then seems to withdraw into an impossibly small point, taking on the form of a man as it does so. Hovering in the air in front of you is a figure dressed in some sickly green material, and with a cloak that looks like it is made of an agglomeration of black spider webs flapping from his shoulders. His skin is sallow, his face split by a lunatic grin, and in one hand he holds a human skull.

"Nightmare!" Moon Knight hisses. "I knew it. Then we are trapped in the Dimension of Dreams, as I feared." He turns to you. "Something must have gone wrong when Doctor Strange cast his portal spell and we were brought here rather than being transported to Egypt."

"That's right!" the Lord of the Nightmare Realm cackles. "You will remain here as my playthings, never to leave."

"Not as long as I have breath in my lungs!" Moon Knight roars and throws himself at the demon.

"Then let's see if I can't take your breath away," Nightmare giggles and prepares to meet the vigilante's attack with more esoteric weapons of his own.

This is a boss fight!

Round one: roll two dice and add your **MIGHT** and your **MIND**, along with any {**SWEET DREAMS**} you may have but deduct any {**FEARFUL**}. If the total is 15 or more, you win the first round.

Round two: roll two dice and add your **MIGHT** and, if you have any, your {**UNLOCKED**} and your {**ECLIPSED**}. If the total is 16 or more, you win the second round.

Round three: roll two dice and add your **MIGHT** and, if you have any, your {**UNLOCKED**} and your {**ECLIPSED**}. If the total is 17 or more, you win the third round.

If you won the third round, turn to **259**.

If you lost the third round, turn to **189**.

220

You hand the Sorcerer Supreme the artifact and he passes you the [Orb of Belgaroth] in return.

"Be warned," Strange says darkly as you make the exchange, "do not reveal to your enemies that you have the Orb until you have no choice other than to use it."

Take +1 {ABRACADABRA}.

An ominous rumble passes through the building, sending dust showering from the ancient volumes lining the shelves of the library.

Turn to **297**.

221

The jackals continue their advance, muscles tensed beneath their sleek black coats, teeth bared as they maintain their threatening guttural rumbling.

"Be still," Moon Knight says softly, shushing the jackals' growls. "I mean you no harm. I am not your enemy. Rest easy, I have no quarrel with you."

Does the avatar of Khonshu have what it takes to subdue the servants of Anubis?

Take +1 {GRANTED} and then make an animal mastery test. Roll one die and add your **MYSTIC** to it. What's the result?

8 or more: turn to **202**.

7 or less: turn to **163**.

222

"Look!" you exclaim, pointing at the spires of the cathedral. "Up there! Could it be…?"

It might be cheesy, but you couldn't think of anything else in the heat of the moment. But cheesy or not, for a split second the Grey Gargoyle falls for your trick and takes his eyes off you. In that moment, you scramble back inside the limousine.

"Driver!" you shout in a panic. "Lock the doors."

There is a click, followed by the electronic voice's response. "*Doors locked.*"

Take +1 **MIND**.

Turn to **241**.

223

You are expecting the vigilante to engage in hand-to-hand combat with the Living Mummy, but instead he tries using a more hi-tech 21st century solution. He calls in a drone strike.

Myriad crescent-shaped drones, each one more than a foot across, sweep down out of the sky on a collision course with N'Kantu's position. Some are deflected by the howling magical winds, but others find their target and detonate on impact.

ACHIEVEMENT: *Overkill.*

Now turn to **252**.

224

Both you and Moon Knight are taken by surprise when something drops out of a tree, almost landing on top of you. It is a muscular, bearded man wearing a flamboyant costume that makes it look like his head and torso are emerging from a roaring lion's mouth.

In his hand he holds a whip, which he cracks as he growls: "The Moon Knight. Are you prey worthy of Sergei Kravinoff?"

"It is not me you should be hunting, Kraven," the Fist of Khonshu states.

And then, fast as a pair of striking cobras, the two hunters engage in battle. As they trade blows, you can see for yourself that Kraven the Hunter is clearly adept at using his whip, while Moon Knight lays about him with his baton with equal aplomb.

This is a tough fight!

Round one: roll two dice and add your **MIGHT**. If the total is 13 or more, you win the first round.

Round two: roll two dice and add your **MIGHT**. If you won the first round, add 1. If the total is 12 or more, you win the second round.

Round three: roll two dice and add your **MIGHT**. If you won the second round, add 1. If the total is 11 or more, you win the third round.

If you won the third round, turn to **108**.

If you lost the third round, turn to **89**.

225

You watch incredulously as the body of Khonshu's Fist goes limp beneath the throttling hands of N'Kantu the Living Mummy.

"There is one who still remains who might yet threaten the completion of your great work," Dr Uraeus addresses Anubis, which takes you aback. His words are almost as shocking as the death of Moon Knight.

"No there isn't," growls the god of the dead, snapping his fingers. His faithful pets leap into action, dragging you to the ground. Fortunately for you, you lose consciousness at that point, and have no awareness of what happens to your body after that.

The End.

226

You're not sure whether the Werewolf's snarling is an antagonistic behavior or if it is a sign of some inner turmoil. But regardless of the truth, the best form of defense is attack.

Acting without hesitation, Moon Knight moves swiftly and lands a blow against the lycanthrope before his adversary can make good on its threat posturing.

Take +1 {UNLOCKED}.

Turn to **70**.

227

The man is dressed in the garb you would imagine a mercenary would wear. He is lying face down in the sand, at the feet of a colossal statue that dominates the temple facade.

Looking up at the figure's face, there is something eerily familiar about it. The skilled craftsmen who created the effigy depicted it as wearing nothing more than a white linen kilt and a pharaoh's headdress. Its face, however, is a blank visage, other than its almond-shaped eyes, which lack pupils. In its hands is a staff surmounted by a crescent moon.

Turning your attention back to the mercenary, you roll him over and are startled when you see how battered and bruised his face is. He has clearly been subjected to a savage beating. He still doesn't move, and you put your fingers to his neck in search of a pulse. It's no good, the man is dead. Take +1 {FEARFUL}.

But are you too late to help him? Perhaps you have something in your possession that could accomplish what would appear to be impossible and revive him.

If you have an [Ankh] and want to use it now, turn to **285**.

If you have the [Black Grimoire] and want to use it now, turn to **295**.

If you have the [Orb of Belgaroth] and want to use it now, turn to **11**.

If you have none of these items, turn to **31**.

228

You cannot see how Frenchie Duchamp can hold back the approaching zombies alone, even if he is a hard-bitten mercenary.

If you think Moon Knight should help him and worry about exploring the temple once the zombies have been dealt with, turn to **151**.

Knowing that time is of the essence, if you think it best to leave Frenchie, as he himself instructed, and enter the subterranean complex, turn to **97**.

229

Moon Knight is too swift and too agile to be repelled by Black Spectre's feeble defense. After all, he has height on his side and the moon behind him to confuse the lawbreaker.

He takes him down without Carson Knowles laying a finger on him. As Black Spectre hits the tarmac, something rolls from his hand, even as a swift punch to the face renders him unconscious.

Take +1 MIND and +1 MIGHT.

Turn to 136.

230

With Moon Knight stunned into inaction, his gaze locked on the canopic jar, N'Kantu the Living Mummy makes his escape, fleeing from the exhibition hall with his prize clutched tightly to his bandage-wrapped chest. Take +1 {AWED}.

Turn to 105.

231

It is no good. There is nothing you can do to save Moon Knight as his life steadily ebbs away. With Khonshu's avatar dead, there is no way you can stop the ritual by yourself, and so every human being on the planet is doomed to become a zombie as the world enters the Age of Anubis.

ACHIEVEMENT: *Gone to the Dogs.*

The End.

232

"I will help you look for Anubis's servant," Shadow Knight says, "but do not think for a minute that this means we are on the same side."

Without waiting for a reply, Moon Knight's dark doppelganger takes off again into the night over the rooftops.

"Do you really think you can trust him?" you ask the vigilante. "You don't think he's working for Anubis, too?"

"My brother may be many things," Moon Knight says, sighing deeply, "but he is loyal to Khonshu, in his own warped way. It is frustrating that we can't see eye-to-eye. However, never forget that the enemy of your enemy is your friend, whether he likes to admit it or not."

You relate to that more than *you'd* like to admit.

Take **+1 {HUNTED}**.

Turn to **106**.

233

Moon Knight is a master of many martial arts disciplines, but N'Kantu the Living Mummy was once a mighty warrior himself, and led a bloody uprising against those who had enslaved his tribe – in short, he knows one or two tricks himself. Not only that, but the arcane alchemical process that has preserved his body for millennia has also imbued the Mummy with superhuman strength and he will not be so easily bested.

This is a fight!

Round one: roll two dice and add your **MIGHT**. If the total is 11 or more, you win the first round.

Round two: roll two dice and add your **MIGHT**. If you won the first round, add 1. If your total is 10 or more, you win the second round.

If you won the second round, turn to **129**.

If you lost the second round, turn to **159**.

234

The door of the house suddenly opens and a voice snaps from within, "Inside! Quickly, before the massed hordes of the undead breach the barrier!"

You and Moon Knight do not need to be told twice and throw yourselves through, as your savior holds back the zombies with an impressive arsenal of combat spells. The Sorcerer Supreme wears a golden talisman, in the shape of an eye, that holds his cloak in place at his neck. He makes a series of occult gestures with his hands. The Eye appears to open, and from it bursts a beam of radiant light that illuminates the length of Bleecker Street, as if it were midday rather than midnight. The attacking hordes visibly falter as they are weakened by its power.

The door slams shut again and Doctor Strange turns his furious gaze upon Moon Knight. "Marc Spector. I was wondering whether you might show up. So, are you the ones responsible for the *Night of the Living Dead* cosplay re-enactment right on my doorstep?"

"We are the ones trying to stop it," Moon Knight rails. "It is N'Kantu the Living Mummy who has brought this plague upon the city."

Roll one die and divide the number rolled by two, rounding fractions up. If the result is less than or equal to your {WHO LET THE DOGS OUT?}, turn to **244**.

If it is greater than your {WHO LET THE DOGS OUT?}, or you have not acquired that particular Quality, roll one die. If the number rolled is less than or equal to your {ABRACADABRA} and {DARK POWER} combined, turn to **257**.

If it is greater than your {ABRACADABRA} and {DARK POWER} combined, or you have not acquired either of those Qualities, turn to **277**.

"Very well," the Werewolf concedes, but he is clearly not happy about it.

Regardless, however, he pads along at Moon Knight's heels as your curious party leaves the protection of the alleyway and, keeping to the areas of shadow that lie between the pools of light cast by a million light bulbs around Times Square, make your way toward the stepped platform.

Lit from underneath, the steps glow red, meaning that N'Kantu is bathed in a crimson glow while the hieroglyphs covering the clay pot are outlined in ruby fire. As you creep toward the steps, you can see the Mummy's desert-dry lips moving, which suggests he is intoning some dark magical spell.

It's time for a stealth minigame!

Round one: roll one die, and add your **MIND** and your **MYSTIC**, and any {ECLIPSED}. Score 8 or more: you win round one.

Round two: roll one die and add your **MIND** and your **MYSTIC**, and any {ECLIPSED}. If you won round one, add +2. On a 9 or more, you win round two.

Did you win round two?

> If so, turn to **274**.
>
> If not, turn to **255**.

236

Two minutes later, you and Moon Knight are standing just outside the Metropolitan Museum of Art. An unending river of traffic makes its way along Fifth Avenue, the white trails of headlamps and the red glow of taillights crisscrossing in the darkness.

Where can the Living Mummy have gone? There are no screams of panic from the public indicating where N'Kantu might be.

"Where would I go if I was an undead monster in the Big Apple at night?" you wonder out loud.

"Somewhere dark," Moon Knight replies, scanning the street.

The streetlights, neon signs, the lighted squares of windows in the surrounding buildings, and the headlights of the vehicles all mean that you can see as well as if it was midday. The only place that has any pockets of darkness nearby is the park behind the museum.

How will you respond?

"We're in the city that never sleeps. Nowhere is dark." Turn to **266**.

"Central Park looks like our best bet." Turn to **296**.

237

Moon Knight hurls the vial at the Mummy and scores a direct hit. The glass shatters, covering the creature with its chemical contents. But it would appear that having flesh almost as hard as stone already makes N'Kantu immune to the Grey Gargoyle's petrification serum.

Strike the [Vial of Serum] from your Inventory, then turn to **13**.

238

"Officer, we are here on official business. The item you can see in my associate's possession is a priceless artifact from the Metropolitan Museum of Art that is under their direct guardianship. It is not a weapon per se."

The cop looks at Mr Knight in bewilderment but keeps his gun trained on you. Take **+1 {GRANTED}**.

"That's as it may be," he says, a waver in his voice, "but I would still like your associate to put the weapon on the floor and step out of the vehicle."

"Ah, Detective Flint," Mr Knight says, addressing a downbeat-looking man in a trench coat who is now approaching the limousine to see what all the fuss is about. "I was just telling this young officer that we are here on official business."

"That's good," the other man says. "I was about to give you a call." He turns to the young police officer. "Put the gun away, son. These people are on our side. And we need allies more than ever."

Mr Knight and Detective Flint stride away toward the roadblock. Thinking it's probably best if you stick together, you leave the [Khopesh] where it is and get out of the car. By the time you catch up with the other two, they are already deep in conversation.

"... right the way down to 52nd Street," you hear the detective say as you join them, his bushy moustache wriggling like a caterpillar as he speaks. "He says he'll trigger the bomb if anyone goes anywhere near him."

"What does he want?" asks Mr Knight.

"I'll give you one guess."

"Me," Mr Knight says, his voice cold.

Eager to be brought up to speed with what's going on, you make an interjection of your own. But what's it to be?

"Who's got a bomb?" Turn to **95**.

"Sounds like you and the bomber have history. Is there bad blood between the two of you, then?" Turn to **55**.

"Sounds like a job for Moon Knight." Turn to **75**.

"What about N'Kantu?" Turn to **154**.

239

Taking the bundle of dynamite in hand, you hurriedly twist the fuses together and light them using the nearest of the burning braziers. Eager to be rid of the fizzing sticks of explosive now, you throw the bundle at the ophidian monster. It lands on the sandy floor close to the serpent and, before the creature can crush them beneath its coils, the [Sticks of Dynamite] explode.

The confined *BOOM!* is loud within the pyramidal space but is quickly replaced by the furious hissing screams of the serpent. The monster is clearly in agony.

Take +2 {SNAKEBITE}, remove the [Sticks of Dynamite] from your Inventory, and make a note that you cannot return to this section again.

Do you have anything else you could use against the Serpent God?

If you do, turn back to **82** and try something you haven't tried previously.

If not, it's time to fight: turn to **192**.

240

The cesti are ancient battle gloves, the Classical World's equivalent of brass knuckledusters. But those that are among the Fist of Khonshu's crime-fighting arsenal have been forged with silver-tipped spikes.

As Mr Knight puts them on you sense a change in the Black Spectre's stance. You suspect that the villain has been on the receiving end of a beating from the vigilante before.

Make an intimidation test. Roll one die and add your **MIGHT** to it. If your total is 7 or more, take **+1 MIGHT**.

And then Mr Knight engages in battle with Black Spectre, but it is a very one-sided fight.

Turn to **291**.

241

The moon god's vengeance given human form, Moon Knight lands on the sidewalk between you and the super villain. Whatever the Grey Gargoyle thought he had done to Moon Knight, it clearly wasn't enough to put him out of action for long.

Without uttering a word, the Fist of Khonshu does what he does best, and punches the Grey Gargoyle square in the face. The stony super villain reels at the blow, but quickly recovers, ready to give as good as he gets.

"So, you would seek to battle the fabulous Grey Gargoyle a second time this night?" Duval asks, with barely suppressed laughter. "This should be most interesting."

This is a tough fight!

Round one: roll two dice and add your **MIGHT**. If the total is 14 or more, you win the first round.

Round two: roll two dice and add your **MIGHT**. If you won the first round, add 1. If the total is 13 or more, you win the second round.

Round three: roll two dice and add your **MIGHT**. If you won the second round, add 1. If the total is 12 or more, you win the third round.

If you won the third round, turn to **29**.

If you lost the third round, turn to **270**.

242

Before too long, you are standing at the entrance to Central Park Zoo. With only a cursory glance to check that no one's around, Moon Knight leaps over the gates, leaving you to clamber up after him. Dropping down on the other side, you follow the white figure of the vigilante as he explores the zoo in search of the Mummy.

You catch up with him at the center of the zoological gardens. "Any sign of N'Kantu?" you ask.

He doesn't need to give you an answer when you hear a deep-throated growling behind you. You slowly turn to see a pair of large jackals stalking toward you, their bodies crouched low. Standing behind them is the Mummy, the canopic jar still in his grasp.

"I didn't know they had jackals at this zoo," you say in a strained whisper, unable to tear your eyes from the savage dogs.

"They might be otherworldly servants of Anubis that N'Kantu has summoned to assist him," Moon Knight replies, keeping his voice low as well.

"They should put that on the placard," you say. "Bring in more tourists."

Moon Knight huffs a soft laugh.

No matter the truth, you are both in danger. Take +1 {WHO LET THE DOGS OUT?}.

The Living Mummy suddenly gives voice to a parched cough. Several seconds of this pass before you realize he is not coughing but laughing, as he retreats into the darkness. Turning tail, he flees from the zoo, just like he did at the museum.

"These animals may be savage, but they are only doing as their master commanded, and N'Kantu is getting away," says Moon Knight. "The longer we delay here the harder it will be for us to catch up with him again."

What do you think Moon Knight should do?

If you think he should try to subdue the jackals, turn to **221**.

If you think it would be wisest to attack the dogs, turn to **182**.

If you think he should ignore the animals and go after N'Kantu, turn to **147**.

243

Clearly the two brothers have nothing more to say to each other and instead engage in a vicious battle, wielding close-combat weapons against each other. Take +1 {UNLOCKED}.

This is a brutal fight!

Round one: roll two dice and add your **MIGHT**. If the total is 15 or more, you win the first round.

Round two: roll two dice and add your **MIGHT**. If you won the first round, add 1. If your total is 15 or more, you win the second round.

If you won the second round, turn to **84**.

If you lost the second round, turn to **176**.

244

"The notorious agent of Anubis," Strange adds. "Do you think the Heliopolitan God of the Dead has sent his servant to harvest the souls of the living in a great swathe for him, then?"

Considering everything you have witnessed, from the initial theft of the canopic jar from the Metropolitan Museum of Art to the ritual the Mummy conducted in Times Square, unleashing the tenth plague of Egypt upon NYC and stealing the souls of those who then rose again as zombies, you cannot come up with a better explanation.

"It would seem so," says Moon Knight. "Perhaps he has grown impatient of waiting for people to die before he can collect their souls and wanted to speed up the process to increase his power. But Khonshu demands vengeance for all those Anubis's servants have attacked this night, and I am the instrument of his vengeance."

Take +1 {ECLIPSED}.

"Gods and monsters, all of them. When will the inhabitants of Celestial Heliopolis learn not to meddle in the affairs of Earth?" Strange grumbles.

"That will never happen, for without the human race, the Heliopolitans are nothing," says Khonshu's Fist.

Make a magic test. Add together any {ABRACADABRA} and {DARK POWER} you may have, then roll one die and if the result is less than or equal to your {ABRACADABRA} and {DARK POWER} combined, turn to **257**.

If it is greater than your {ABRACADABRA} and {DARK POWER} combined, or you have not acquired either of those Qualities, turn to **277**.

245

"It was N'Kantu who stole the canopic jar from the museum in the first place," you tell Moon Knight. "If it wasn't for him, we wouldn't be in this mess right now."

"That barbarian warlord has lived long enough!" the vigilante snaps, maintaining the same strong NYC drawl. "It's time he was put down once and for all."

With that, Moon Knight swoops across the chamber on the wings of his outstretched cloak, ready to battle the Living Mummy one last time.

This is going to be a tough fight!

Round one: roll two dice and add your **MIGHT**, along with your {**UNLOCKED**}. If the total is 20 or more, you win the first round.

Round two: roll two dice and add your **MIGHT**, along with your {**UNLOCKED**}. If you won round one, add 1. If the total is 21 or more, you win the second round.

Round three: roll two dice and add your **MIGHT**, along with your {**UNLOCKED**}. If you won round two, add 2. If the total is 22 or more, you win the third round.

Subtract 1 from the number of rounds you won and adjust your **MIGHT** by that much: this could range from **+2** if you won all three, to **-1** if you lost all three.

> If you won round three, you have defeated the Living Mummy, but are not out of danger yet: turn to **261**.
>
> If you lost round three, turn to **225**.

246

The Werewolf keeps up his snarling, shooting glances to left and right, as if he is afraid of something, but he doesn't attack.

Make a vigilante test. Roll one die.

> If it is equal to or less than your {**UNLOCKED**}, turn immediately to **226**.

If it is greater than your {UNLOCKED}, or you do not have any, you consider how best to deal with the wolfman. What do you want to use?

An [Ankh], if you have one: turn to **28**.

A [Tactical Grenade], if you have one: turn to **14**.

A [Khopesh], if you have one: turn to **121**.

A [Whip], if you have one: turn to **73**.

A [Vial of Serum], if you have one: turn to **87**.

Try calming the Werewolf down: turn to **46**.

247

"Hello?" you call out, your voice acquiring an eerie quality as it carries over the silent desert. "Can you hear me? Are you all right? Hello?"

The man doesn't respond and doesn't even move in response to your voice. Take **+1** {FEARFUL}.

What do you want to try now?

Approach the man to check on him: turn to **227**.

Do nothing and watch to see what might happen: turn to **265**.

Something suddenly detaches itself from a flying buttress, as if one of the statues that adorn the building has come to life, and you give an involuntary gasp of surprise.

"Grey Gargoyle!" Moon Knight shouts. "I don't have time to deal with you tonight."

"Then you must make time," the other declares, in a thick French accent, "for the fabulous Grey Gargoyle could do with a workout!"

"We really don't have time for this," Moon Knight reiterates, looking to you as if for moral support. "Do we?"

What do you think Moon Knight should do?

> If you think he should attack the Grey Gargoyle, turn to **44**.
>
> If you think he should call on Khonshu for aid, turn to **155**.
>
> If you think he should use the precarious nature of your surroundings to help him, turn to **63**.

Rather than take a swipe at Moon Knight with his sword, at the last second Black Spectre twists out of the way. The only thing the Fist of Khonshu makes contact with is the tarmac. Take **-1 MIGHT**.

The vigilante is on his feet again in seconds and dives at the villain. But his opponent has dropped his weapons and now has something else gripped in his right hand. It appears to be an explosive device of some kind, and Knowles's thumb is hovering over the trigger.

Make a speed test. Roll one die and add your **MIGHT**. What's the result?

Total of 8 or more: turn to **116**.

7 or less: turn to **156**.

"Khonshu, I have done what you wanted," Moon Knight suddenly cries. "Do not forsake your son now!"

With a tectonic heave, part of the roof of the chamber comes crashing down not two yards from where you are standing, while a rift zigzags across the ground and part of the floor cantilevers upward. The total collapse of the chamber is only moments away.

Suddenly, light floods the vault again. It emanates from a triangular doorway that has just opened in mid air. Framed within it you believe you can make out a figure clad in what might be the robes of a priest but could also be bandages. In its hand it holds a staff, topped with a crescent moon, while the figure's head doesn't appear to be quite all there. In fact, you could swear it doesn't have a head at all, and instead a huge bird's skull hovers in the air over the place where its neck should be.

"This way!" Moon Knight shouts, running for the triangle of light. As he vanishes into it, you and Frenchie follow.

For a moment you feel like you are bathed in moonlight so bright that it blinds you. But then the sensation passes, and you open your eyes to find yourself in almost total darkness. Only the glow of emergency lightning offers any illumination, and you look around in disbelief at the broken display cabinets and missing artifacts.

You are back in the ancient Egyptian gallery, standing in the middle of the devastated exhibition space, but there is no sign of either Moon Knight or Frenchie.

ACHIEVEMENT: *Fast Travel*.

You might have saved the world and restored those who had been transformed into mindless horrors by the zombie plague N'Kantu unleashed upon the city, but that doesn't change the fact that you are going to have a lot of explaining to do come the morning. Not least of which will be enlightening HR regarding the sudden absence of Dr Uraeus, the museum's curator.

ACHIEVEMENT: *Awkward Questions*.

Final score: 3 stars.

The End.

251

The Ankh is also known as the Key of Life and is shown on countless tomb paintings and illuminated papyrus scrolls being touched to the lips of dead pharaohs, in order to restore them to life in the hereafter, once they have passed over to the West Bank of the Nile.

It's got to be worth a try, right?

You take the [Ankh] and, mimicking those shaven-headed, leopard skin-wearing priests of long ago, you touch the artifact to Moon Knight's mouth. For a moment, you are sure the golden object glows more brightly in the inconstant, flickering torchlight. But then the glow fades and the [Ankh] appears to have dulled in color. It looks more like lead than gold now.

Your selfless act has drained the [Ankh] of its divine power and it will no longer be of any use to you. Strike the [Ankh] from your Inventory but take the ACHIEVEMENT: *Life Saver*.

However, it was not a foolish act, since the Key of Life has done precisely what you had hoped it would do. It has restored Moon Knight's health. Take **+6 MIGHT**.

He sits up, looking at you with a bewildered expression.

"Thank you... I think," he says, once he's pulled his mask back in place. "I sense that we are closing in on the place where the ritual is being performed. We must press on. We cannot let anything else delay us now."

Turn to **264**.

252

The spiraling winds abruptly increase in force, rising to hurricane levels in no time at all, and you struggle to find something to hang onto, lest you be carried away by the magical gale.

Fighting to keep your eyes open in the face of the wind, you nonetheless witness a portal swell into being at the eye of the storm. One moment the Mummy is there, the next he has gone. Before Moon Knight can follow him through, the wind drops again, just as suddenly, and the portal snaps shut.

N'Kantu, the agent of Anubis, has escaped and taken the cursed canopic jar of Akharis with him.

Take the ACHIEVEMENT: *Mummy's Boy.*

Turn to **10**.

253

You hold your talisman up between you and the monster. The serpent's gaze fixes on the [Eye of Horus] and it lets out an angry hiss, its long tongue darting from between its huge fangs in irritation.

Take +1 {SNAKEBITE} and make a note that you cannot return to this section.

Do you have anything else you could use against the serpent god?

If you do, turn back to **82** and try something you haven't tried previously.

If not, it's time to fight: turn to **192**.

254

His muscles bunching under his bodyglove, Moon Knight channels all the power that he possesses into freeing himself from the bandages binding him. There is a sound like a bedsheet being torn in half, and then the vigilante is free once more. Take **+1 MIGHT**.

Turn to **281**.

255

Your small party begins to move stealthily across the plaza when N'Kantu suddenly catches sight of you. But he doesn't stop muttering the words of whatever spell it is he is intoning. Instead, he points the open mouth of the canopic jar in your direction and a bolt of dark energy leaps from it. All three of you are sent flying.

Take -1 MIGHT, -1 MIND, -1 MYSTIC, and +2 {AWED}.

The three of you pick yourselves up, Moon Knight brushing the dirt from his white cloak, while Jack Russell pats at patches of smoldering fur.

With a shout that echoes across Times Square and has everyone looking in his direction, N'Kantu completes his incantation. You half expect another manifestation of dark power to burst from the jar, but instead an eerie silence falls over the plaza.

Suddenly, and entirely unexpectedly, roughly half the people from the Renaissance Hotel at the north end of the square to Times Square tower at the south, drop to the ground, as if they were marionettes and somebody had come along and cut their strings.

You wonder if it is just the glow of the streetlights or a result of your heightened state of mind, but it seems to you that shapeless tendrils of mist are rising from the bodies of the fallen and streaming through the air, before ultimately entering the open mouth of the canopic jar. But the weirdness doesn't end there.

As you watch, the people who just collapsed get back to their feet. But now they move with a strange jerkiness and leave any possessions they had been carrying where they dropped them. It would appear that they are more interested in the other people who are watching in disbelief at what is unfolding, as you are. Take +1 {AWED}.

Someone screams and you see a middle-aged Latina lady topple to the ground as a young man wearing a backpack leaps on her and sinks his teeth into her shoulder. Just as quickly as he attacked her, he abandons her prone form, in search of another victim. But barely have you had time to take another breath before the woman gets to her feet again only to fall upon a startled Japanese tourist, snapping at his throat with slavering jaws. And then the scene explodes into violence.

You've seen enough late night double features to know what's happening. The population of NYC is under attack from zombies! And you are right in the thick of things.

"This doesn't change anything," says Moon Knight, seeing the expression of slack-jawed horror on your face. "We have to stop N'Kantu."

With that, he throws himself into the fray, leaving you and Jack with no choice but to follow.

Achievement: *Night of the Living Dead.*

Turn to **299**.

256

It's no good. Despite having what you would have thought was the advantage, you soon lose sight of the other as he bounds and dives from one building to another, eventually vanishing into one of the dark canyons that lie between the looming towers of the metropolis. Take **-1 MIND**.

"Next time, brother," Moon Knight mutters under his breath. "But tonight the Moon Knight has other prey, for there is another who must face Khonshu's vengeance."

Turn to **106**.

257

"A portion of the power of the Darkhold has been unleashed within the city this night," says Doctor Strange. "There was a great perturbation in the ether and the daemonic choirs of Hell sang out in unison while nightmares ran amok within the Dimension of Dreams and the voices of the damned cried out to me."

A shiver of primal fear passes through your body at the mere mention of the name "Darkhold."

Take **+1 {GRANTED}** and then turn to **277**.

258

Without engaging in any pleasantries first, and foregoing any snappy one-liners, Mr Knight sets about him with his baton. It is only then that you notice the mysterious, but sinister-looking, matte black device that Black Spectre has gripped tightly in one hand.

Turn to **116.**

Moon Knight is assailed by one nightmarish vision after another, his adversary manipulating the very fabric of the Nightmare Realm to serve his needs. But the Fist of Khonshu beats back each and every one, bringing all the weapons in his arsenal to bear, as well as all his martial arts skills. As he fights, his body starts to glow, bright as the moon itself, until a beam of blinding energy bursts from the crescent on his chest.

Under the intense beam of moonlight, the demon's final hideous apparition is banished, leaving only Nightmare, whose body in turn seems to be burned away as the light of the moon leaves no shadows for him to hide in.

With a final agonizing cry, the Lord of the Nightmare Realm is banished, and you are forced to close your eyes against the intensity of the searing light.

But when you open them again mere moments later, you can see a brilliant blue cloudless sky above you and now it is the brightness of the sun that makes you squint.

You sit up. You are in the Dimension of Dreams no longer. By defeating Nightmare, Moon Knight has freed you both from the unreal realm. He is standing there before you now, offering you a hand, ready to help you to your feet. It is a hand you gladly accept.

"It this Egypt?" you ask hesitantly.

"Where else would we be?" challenges Moon Knight.

You look around you, taking in every point of the compass. You can literally see nothing but sand in every direction, but at least this sand is yellow. It feels exciting to return to a country you have visited many times during your career as an Egyptologist, but on all those previous occasions you didn't travel anywhere as isolated as this.

A familiar booming voice suddenly echoes within your skull, making you cry out in alarm. *Seek out the temple Akharis built to honor his dark master!*

Judging from Moon Knight's startled reaction, he heard the voice too.

"I take it this isn't actually the location of the temple that Akharis instructed to be built," you say, as the echo fades.

"No," Moon Knight confirms. "I suspect it will be in the mountains somewhere."

"In which case, how are we going to get there? I doubt I could make it much further than the horizon in this heat and without water," you point out.

"Don't worry," Moon Knight says, and you can detect a wry tone in his voice. "I know a guy." With that, he speaks into the communicator attached to his wrist. "Spector calling Jean-Paul Duchamp. Moon Knight calling Jean-Paul Duchamp. Frenchie, pick up. It's Marc."

Accompanied by the crackle of static, a thickly accented voice comes back over the radio transmitter.

"Marc Spector? *Mon ami*, it is good to hear from you again. Are you in Egypt?"

"I am."

"Thank God for that. We need your help! *Mon dieu*, but this place is going mad." This Frenchie's agitation is evident, even over the crackling airwaves. "There are zombies everywhere and their numbers are growing all the time as more and more people succumb to the plague they carry."

"That's why I'm here. But first I need your help. Can you pick us up?"

"Us? But of course, once I take down a few more of these undead. Send me your coordinates."

Turn to **279**.

260

Before we continue with the adventure, let's set up the powers for Moon Knight and you, the Egyptologist. There are three core stats, **MIGHT**, **MYSTIC**, and **MIND**. You remember that from the introduction, which you absolutely read, yeah? Hm.

Might represents Moon Knight's current strength, agility, and resilience. Very helpful for punching things, which will turn out to be useful any moment now, as well as throwing things, leaping over things, breaking things, and all sorts of other tasks you'll encounter in due course.

Mystic is a measure of how persuasive other people consider Moon Knight to be at the time, but it also has a supernatural element to it. It can be affected by events that might impact other people's perceptions, and by acts of the gods.

Mind indicates your team's current level of mental ability. It's handy for solving problems, spotting objects that are out of the way or hard to notice and thinking up clever solutions on the fly. However, you'll still have to solve the puzzles in this book on your own.

Your core stats will change repeatedly over the course of your adventure, so you'll need to keep track of them on a piece of paper or a digital equivalent. You start with **MIGHT** of 2, **MYSTIC** of 2, and **MIND** of 3.

Right – back to the action…

As you are distracted by the arrival of the vigilante, the Living Mummy snatches the [Canopic Jar] from your grasp. Remove it from your Inventory.

When Moon Knight realizes what your bandaged assailant is holding in his withered hands he freezes in shock. "N'Kantu," he gasps. "What are you doing with that?"

Make a willpower test. Roll one die and add your **MYSTIC** and **MIND** to it. What's the result?

Total of 8 or more: turn to **179**.

7 or less: turn to **230**.

261

"The one who is actually behind all this, who has caused you so much pain, is Anubis, god of the dead," you tell your companion.

"God of the dead?" Moon Knight – or should that be Jake Lockley? – scoffs. "More like the god who shall be dead!"

With that he launches himself at the dog-headed deity. But as he swoops across the chamber, his crescent moon cloak outstretched like a pair of wings behind him, with barely a word from Anubis, the jackals attack.

Moon Knight will have to deal with the graveyard guardians quickly if he is to stop Anubis.

Round one: roll two dice and add your **MIGHT**, along with your {**UNLOCKED**}. If the total is 14 or more, you win the first round.

Round two: roll two dice and add your **MIGHT**, along with your {**UNLOCKED**}. If the total is 15 or more, you win the second round.

If you won the second round, turn to **196**.

If you lost the second round, turn to **214**.

262

While Moon Knight is distracted by events unfolding below on Fifth Avenue, something detaches itself from a flying buttress and pounces. It is as if one of the statues that adorn the building has suddenly come to life.

"Grey Gargoyle!" Moon Knight cries out as he fends off a blow from the costumed super villain.

"Yes, the fabulous Grey Gargoyle!" the other declares, in a thick French accent. "It would seem that your moon god has abandoned you, Fist of Khonshu, for this is the last night you will ever see!"

This is a tough fight!

Round one: roll two dice, add your **MIGHT**, and subtract your {**IN THE HEIGHTS**}. If the total is 14 or more, you win the first round.

Round two: roll two dice, add your **MIGHT**, and subtract your {**IN THE HEIGHTS**}. If the total is 13 or more, you win the second round.

Round three: roll two dice, add your **MIGHT**, and subtract your {**IN THE HEIGHTS**}. If the total is 12 or more, you win the third round.

If you won the third round, turn to **29**.

If you lost the third round, turn to **270**.

263

"Officer," he says, taking a step toward the cop, "the thing is, we don't have time for this."

What happens next moves so quickly that neither you nor the policeman know what's going on until the young man is doubled up, clutching his stomach and retching, while his gun is somehow now in Mr Knight's hand. In one deft movement, Mr Knight ejects the magazine, and the chambered round that was already in the gun, before handing the empty firearm back to the police officer.

"Is that Detective Flint over there?" Mr Knight asks and strides toward the roadblock without waiting for an answer.

Deciding it's probably best if you stick together, you get out of the car, carefully stepping over the cop who is on his knees now, gasping for breath, and head after the dapper vigilante. Take **+1 {UNLOCKED}** and **+1 {FEARED}**.

By the time you catch up with Mr Knight, he is already in conversation with a downbeat-looking man wearing a trench coat.

"... right the way down to 52nd Street," you hear the detective say as you join them, his bushy moustache wriggling like a caterpillar as he speaks. "He says he'll trigger the bomb if anyone goes anywhere near him."

"What does he want, Flint?" asks Mr Knight.

"I'll give you one guess."

"Me," Mr Knight says, his voice cold.

"I was about to give you a call," adds Detective Flint.

Eager to be brought up to speed with what's going on, you make an interjection of your own. But what's it to be?

"Who's got a bomb?" Turn to **95**.

"Sounds like you and the bomber have history. Is there bad blood between the two of you?" Turn to **55**.

"Sounds like a job for Moon Knight." Turn to **75**.

"What about N'Kantu?" Turn to **154**.

264

Another dressed stone passageway proceeds ever deeper into the mountain with more torches in sconces providing basic illumination. Not seeing that you have much choice, you and your companion make your way along it.

You have not gone far when you come across an opening in the wall to your left. Peering through it, you discover another chamber with walls adorned with carvings of ancient Egyptian deities and the ever present hieroglyphs. On the far side is a plinth, on top of which stands an exquisite Eye of Horus amulet. It sparkles where the flickering firelight from the torches catches the gleaming gold and luxurious lapis lazuli.

Moon Knight barely gives it a second glance, but the presence of the artifact, untouched and seemingly unguarded, intrigues you. Not only that, but considering what you are likely about to face, it might be of use, since the Eye of Horus was a potent symbol of protection for the ancient Egyptians.

If you want to enter the chamber to retrieve the Eye of Horus, turn to **284**.

If you would rather ignore it, turn to **98**.

265

The facade of the temple is adorned with towering pillars fashioned to resemble stylized papyrus plants, carvings of serpent-bound discs, and endless hieroglyphs. But it is dominated by the statue of a colossal figure.

There is something eerily familiar about the figure's features, which are picked out by the moonlight that shines upon it. The skilled craftsmen who created the statue have depicted it as wearing nothing more than a cloth skirt and a pharaoh's headdress. Its face, however, is a blank visage, other than its almond-shaped eyes, which lack pupils. In its hands is a staff surmounted by a crescent moon.

The mercenary is lying at the feet of this statue.

Moonlight bathes the stone-carved god, making its face glow, and you hear a voice carry to you across the desert that you hear both outside and inside your head.

Marc? Marc Spector, can you hear me? Come to me, my son, and be reborn in my light.

You are surprised to see the man stir at the sound of the voice and push himself up out of the sand. His voice now carries to you over the sands, but it is not you whom he is addressing when he says, "Who are you?"

You have a choice, Marc Spector, the voice comes again. *Do you want death, or do you want life?*

"I… I want to live," the man replies.

Then you will be mine. You will be my hands. My eyes. My vengeance. You will be my knight.

Take **+1 MYSTIC**.

Turn to **31**.

266

"There is always darkness in men's hearts, and therefore there will always be those who travel by night who need my protection," Moon Knight replies.

Rather than race off down the steps, the Fist of Khonshu bows his head and whispers, "Khonshu, greatest of the great gods, show me the way."

And then you jump as you hear the ethereal voice of Khonshu again, but whether it is inside your head or in the air around you, you cannot tell.

N'Kantu will not enact the ritual until he is in a place where it will have the greatest effect.

Moon Knight is quiet for a moment before declaring, "Times Square! Of course! Even at this time of night it will be bustling with people."

"And somewhere that is the exact opposite of any place that's considered *dark*," you can't help pointing out.

What ritual is Moon Knight talking about, and how can you hear an ancient Egyptian deity talking to the super hero in the first place?

"Come on," Moon Knight says, addressing you again, but then hesitates. "But should we go high or stay low?"

He fixes you with narrowed eyes. Is this some kind of test?

What do you think the two of you should do?

"Go high." Turn to **42**.

"Stay low." Turn to **170**.

267

At long last, you reach 177A Bleecker Street. The grand, three-story Victorian brownstone on the corner of Fenno Place has a reputation among the local populace for being haunted. But it is precisely because it is a focus for otherworldly energies that Doctor Stephen Strange adopted it as his residence and made it his base of operations.

The house is alive with magic and is safeguarded by numerous wards of protection, to stop external threats, supernatural or otherwise, from breaking in, and even worse entities from breaking out. Moon Knight staggers up the steps to the front door and gives the handle a tug, only to be confronted by those very same wards.

Esoteric magical symbols ripple with an eerie green light as the vigilante tries the door. You watch as the sigils form briefly before fading again. Each one appears in the form of a circle. Lines of power crisscross the circles, connecting six equidistant points on the circumference of each one. No two are exactly the same but, as the visual manifestations of the warding runes come and go, you try to count exactly how many there are.

The zombified populace of Greenwich Village is closing on you from both ends of Bleecker Street and it can only be a matter of time before they have you trapped. With nowhere left to run, you must find a way into Doctor Strange's Sanctum Sanctorum. Take **+3 {SANDS OF TIME}**.

What do you want to do?

Knock on the door: turn to **94**.

Call out to the Sorcerer Supreme: turn to **67**.

Try reciting one of the spells contained within the Egyptian Book of the Dead from memory: turn to **104**.

Try uttering an incantation, such as the one you heard N'Kantu intoning: turn to **164**.

Try using an [Ankh], if you have one: turn to **124**.

Try using a [Tactical Grenade], if you have one: turn to **144**.

Try using a [Crossbow], if you have one: turn to **47**.

Try using an [Alien Device], if you have one: turn to **198**.

Call in a drone strike: turn to **184**.

Do nothing and wait: turn to **218**.

268

"Go!" you exclaim. "You have to stop N'Kantu and recover the canopic jar! I'll deal with the Werewolf," you finish, feeling significantly less confident than your bold boast might suggest.

With the Mummy almost within his grasp, Moon Knight doesn't argue, but performs an acrobatic leap over the Werewolf's head, keen to capture his quarry at last.

Still snarling, the Werewolf ignores you and launches into the air, grabbing Moon Knight around the waist and slamming him into the fire escape. The two of them fall back to the ground, landing with a splash in a filthy puddle. Take **-1 MIGHT**.

Turn to **70**.

269

Taking the vial you accidentally acquired from the Grey Gargoyle, you hurl it at the stone giant. The container hits a granite leg and shatters, covering the carved limb in the serum – but it has no effect.

What did you think a serum that turns flesh to stone would do to a body that is already made of stone? Take **+1 {FEARFUL}**.

Turn to **149**.

270

Moon Knight takes quite a beating from the stone-hard fists of the Grey Gargoyle. Even when he lays a kick or a punch against his opponent, the villain's rocky hide causes the vigilante more pain than he manages to deliver. Take **-1 MIGHT**.

"See? I told you, did I not? No one can defeat the Grey Gargoyle!" Duval declares, assuming a suitably triumphant pose.

Turn to **79**.

271

Moon Knight stops rocking and rises to his feet, his mental battle over.

"Marc, are you all right?" you ask.

Moon Knight turns his blazing gaze upon you, and you feel a primal shiver of fear akin to the sensation of ice water trickling down your spine. More importantly, you no longer feel safe.

"Not Marc," he says, his voice an unfamiliar New Yorker drawl, like that favored by drivers of yellow taxi cabs, "Jake, Jake Lockley. And I'm in the mood to share my pain with someone."

Moon Knight bunches his fists and you worry he is going to share his pain with *you*. But there are three others present whom the psychotic vigilante could channel his energies into battling. Which name do you want to give him?

Anubis: turn to **261**.

N'Kantu, the Living Mummy: turn to **245**.

Dr Uraeus: turn to **54**.

272

Anything could have set the animals off, and Moon Knight seems to know where he's going, so you stick to the path you are already following. It leads you to a line of trees that have lost all definition in the darkness, beneath which even darker shadows have gathered.

Make an awareness test. Roll one die and add your **MIND** to it.

6 or more: turn to **204**.

5 or less: turn to **224**.

273

Undoing the silver clasps that hold the book shut, you let the Black Grimoire fall open wherever it chooses. As the pages settle into place, your eyes alight on a spell entitled *"A Charme Against Snakes, Serpents, Basilisks and Amphisbaenas,"* and you begin to read.

The effect is almost instantaneous, the monstrous reptile lashing its body from side to side and twisting itself in knots, just as if it had been thrown on a fire.

Take +1 {SNAKEBITE} and +1 {DARK POWER}, then make a note that you may not return to this section.

Do you have anything else you could use against the Serpent God?

> If you do, turn back to **82** and try something you haven't tried already.
>
> If not, it's time to fight: turn to **192**.

274

Your small party creeps stealthily across the plaza toward N'Kantu, but before you can reach him, with an abrupt shout he concludes his ritual.

An unnerving silence falls like a shroud over Times Square. Suddenly, and entirely unexpectedly, roughly half the people from the Renaissance Hotel at the north end of the square to Times Square tower at the south, drop to the ground, just as if they were marionettes and somebody has come along and cut their strings.

You wonder if it is just the glow of the streetlights or a result of your heightened state of mind, but it seems to you that shapeless tendrils of mist leave the bodies of the fallen and stream through the air into the open mouth of the canopic jar, the hieroglyphs covering it glowing redly, as if lit from within.

The weirdness doesn't end there. As you watch, the people who just collapsed get back to their feet. But now they move with a strange jerkiness and leave any possessions they had been carrying where they dropped them. It would appear that they are more interested in the other people who are watching in disbelief at what is unfolding, as you are. Take +1 {AWED}.

Someone screams and you see a middle-aged Latina lady topple to the ground as a young man wearing a backpack leaps on her and sinks his teeth into her shoulder. Just as quickly as he attacked her, he abandons her prone form, in search of another victim. But barely have you had time to take another breath before the woman gets to her feet again, only to fall upon a startled Japanese tourist, snapping at his throat with slavering jaws. The same thing is happening all across Times Square.

You've seen enough late night double features to know what's happening. The population of NYC is under attack from zombies! And you are right in the thick of things.

ACHIEVEMENT: *Late Night Double Feature.*

"What do we do now?" you hiss under your breath.

"Prepare to fight?" Turn to **299**.

"Act like we've already been turned?" Turn to **288**.

275

Arming himself with a pair of his favored crescent-shaped weapons, while there is still some distance between the two old foes, Mr Knight lets them fly.

It is only then that you notice the mysterious but sinister-looking, matte black device Black Spectre has gripped tightly in one hand.

Make an astonishment test. Roll one die, add your MIND, and subtract your {AWED}.

On a 7 or more: turn to **291**.

6 or less: turn to **116**.

276

"We have both served Khonshu in our time," he goes on, "and now, more than ever, we should be working together to stop Anubis's agent, N'Kantu the Living Mummy, from unleashing hell on New York City."

"The Living Mummy is loose in the Big Apple?"

"Yes, and he has the canopic jar of King Akharis from the Metropolitan Museum of Art."

"For what purpose?" Shadow Knight asks.

"I am unsure, but it cannot be anything good. Will you help me look for him, brother?"

Take +1 {ECLIPSED}.

Turn to **232**.

277

"It is quite clear that whatever N'Kantu began here is far from over," says the sorcerer.

"As long as he is in possession of the cursed canopic jar of King Akharis it will never be over," Moon Knight replies.

"And while that remains the case, things will only get worse."

"He could be anywhere, right now, enacting his evil ritual again and again, until this zombie plague outbreak overtakes the whole planet."

"Then we must find N'Kantu and stop him!" you declare with rising agitation.

"You can do that, can't you, Strange?" says Moon Knight in a way that suggests he already knows the answer.

"Of course I can," the Sorcerer Supreme replies, sounding almost offended. "With the correct magical procedure, I can locate anyone on the planet, or off it."

If you have {NOISY NEIGHBOURS} of 2 or more, turn to **297**.

If not, turn to 7.

278

Unslinging the [Crossbow] from your shoulder, you hastily load a bolt into the flight groove and loose it at the statue. It flies through the air and strikes the granite torso

of the stone giant... but then bounces off harmlessly. Take
+1 {FEARFUL}.

Turn to **149**.

279

Incredibly, within half an hour, you hear the *chukka-chukka-chukka* of a helicopter and, looking to the sky, you see a dark speck approaching your position. It sets down nearby, kicking up great clouds of sand.

Within moments you are being introduced to Jean-Paul "Frenchie" Duchamp – a lean, mercenary type with matinee idol looks and a pencil moustache – and not long after that the three of you are airborne.

"Not like you to be traveling with a civilian, Marc," says Frenchie, his voice sounding tinny through the headset you've been given.

"You'd be surprised just how useful an Egyptologist can be," Moon Knight replies and proceeds to fill his friend in as quickly as he can. In turn, Frenchie tells you how the zombie plague has reached Egypt.

"I was part of a team protecting a dig site in the Akh'ran Highlands," he says. "Only this morning half the workers seemed to drop dead – all of sudden, for no obvious reason… but they didn't stay dead for long! It was all I could do to get to the chopper and take off to pick you up. So where is it we're heading?"

If you know the coordinates of the hidden temple you seek, add the main digits together and turn to the section with the same number as the total.

If you have not discovered the required coordinates, make a devotee test. Roll two dice, and add your **MYSTIC**, as well as any {**ECLIPSED**} you might have. What's the result?

Total of 20 or more: turn to **208**.

19 or less: turn to **188**.

280

The two of you make your way to the edge of Times Square, peering out from the mouth of the alley peer at the neon-lit plaza.

There, standing at the top of the stepped platform that forms the roof of the TKTS discount ticket booth at the center of the Square – which is still filled with revelers and tourists, even at this time of night – is N'Kantu the Living Mummy.

Revelers nearby are so caught up with themselves, taking selfies and posing for videos, that they barely even register his presence. Either that or they think he's a pro cosplayer. Or maybe he is drawing on the dark power of the canopic jar to mask his presence here.

You can feel waves of malign energy emanating from the ancient artifact even at this distance. It makes your skin crawl and your neurons fizz, as if your very DNA is being rewritten the longer you are exposed to it.

"We have to stop him!" you groan, teeth gritted against the pain. "And fast!"

"But N'Kantu doesn't know we're here," Moon Knight points out. "We have the element of surprise, which gives us the advantage. We should use stealth to make our approach."

But before you can act, with a sudden shout, N'Kantu concludes his ritual.

An unnatural silence falls like a shroud over Times Square. A single heartbeat after that, roughly half the people, from the Renaissance Hotel at the north end of the square to Times Square Tower at the south, drop to the ground like marionettes and somebody had come along and cut their strings.

Is it just a trick of the light, or a tired mind, or can you really see shapeless tendrils of mist leave the bodies of the fallen and stream through the air, ultimately entering the open mouth of the canopic jar, while the hieroglyphs covering it glow red, as if from within?

If you have {ABRACADABRA} of 1, turn to **17**.

If not, make an arcane knowledge test: roll one dice, add your **MYSTIC** and your {GRANTED}, if you have any.

If the total is 9 or more, turn to **17**.

If it is 8 or less, turn to **39**.

281

Moon Knight grabs hold of the Mummy's hands and, using his opponent's own weight against him, hurls his attacker over his shoulder. The Living Mummy lands hard on the marble floor... but is on his feet again in moments.

"N'Kantu," Moon Knight growls, "what are you doing here?"

The Living Mummy doesn't answer but launches himself at the vigilante instead.

This is a fight!

Round one: roll one die and add your **MIGHT**. If the total is 7 or more, you win the first round.

Round two: roll one die and add your **MIGHT**. If you won the first round, add 1. If your total is 8 or more, you win the second round.

If you won the second round, turn to **129**.

If you lost the second round, turn to **159**.

282

Access to the Sanctum Sanctorum remains regrettably barred to you, for the time being at least.

Take **-1 {SANDS OF TIME}**, and if you now have a **{SANDS OF TIME}** of zero, turn to **218**.

If not, what do you want to try next?

Knock on the door: turn to **94**.

Call out to the Sorcerer Supreme: turn to **67**.

Try reciting one of the spells from the Egyptian Book of the Dead: turn to **104**.

Try uttering an incantation, such as the one you heard N'Kantu intoning: turn to **164**.

Try using an **[Ankh]**, if you have one: turn to **124**.

Try using a **[Tactical Grenade]**, if you have one: turn to **144**.

Try using a **[Crossbow]**, if you have one: turn to **47**.

Try using an **[Alien Device]**, if you have one: turn to **198**.

Call in a drone strike: turn to **184**.

Do nothing and wait: turn to **218**.

283

"Very well, let's do this," you tell the vigilante.

Moon Knight takes out his baton and launches the grappling hook that is built into it. Traveling on a column of compressed air, the cable flies through the air, over the void, and the anchor ends up lodged in a crevice above the ledge.

Holding the baton tightly in his right hand and putting his other arm around you, the super hero hurls you both into the void.

Make a heights test. Roll two dice, add your **MIGHT**, but deduct any {IN THE HEIGHTS} you might have, if any. What's the result?

Total of 10 or more: turn to **58**.

9 or less: turn to **78**.

284

"Moon Knight, wait!" you hiss, then proceed to enter the chamber.

You walk past the frozen images of the Ennead, locked in stone for all eternity, your attention focused fully on the artifact in front of you. It is an incredible piece, a true work of art that fills you with reverent awe. Take **+1 {AWED}**.

Reaching the plinth, you lift the [Eye of Horus] from its resting place, even as Moon Knight throws himself at you screaming, "No! Don't touch it!" But he's too late.

A great block of stone crashes down, blocking the short tunnel by which you entered and trapping you both inside.

Take the ACHIEVEMENT: *Tomb Raider*.

"What have you *done*?" Moon Knight roars. You have never seen him so angry, even when he was battling N'Kantu. Before you can answer, he sets about trying to shift the stone that has so effectively sealed off the chamber, but it is to no avail.

"I'm sure there must be a secret door or some other way of getting out of here," you say, trying to remain calm, and start to scour the walls for any clues as to how you might get out. There are three holes in the wall next to the entrance.

"I'd rather take my chances against Anubis than be buried alive," Moon Knight mutters.

"It could be worse. You could be buried alive as a zombie," you feel compelled to point out. Your eyes alight on the plinth once more. "What about this?"

Resting upon it are three blocks of stone that were previously hidden behind the [Eye of Horus]. Examining them you see that each one bears a hieroglyph on one of its flat faces while the opposite face is carved into an intricate pattern that reminds you of a stone key. And each one is different. "Could this be the way to get out?"

Moon Knight looks at the three keys and then the three holes in the wall. "It could be. Well spotted. But what is the correct combination?"

It is as you are making your examination that a stone lever set high into the wall above you cantilevers upward, opening a hole in the ceiling, from which sand then starts to pour into the room. As if being imprisoned for all eternity wasn't bad enough, instead you are going to be buried alive in just a few moments.

The three hieroglyphs represented are two reeds, one reed, and a folded piece of cloth (no reeds).

If you can work out the order in which they should be arranged, turn immediately to the appropriate section.

If the correct combination remains a mystery to you, maybe there is something else you could use to help you break out of your prison.

If you have a [Whip], turn to 6.

If you have a [Tactical Grenade], turn to 26.

If you have some [Sticks of Dynamite], turn to 38.

If you have none of these things, your fate is to be buried alive within the subterranean temple...

The End.

285

You touch the golden [Ankh] to the mercenary's wounds but they do not magically start to heal, as you had hoped. Finally, you touch the artifact to his mouth, then sit back on your heels, not knowing what else to do and feeling dejected that your curious ministrations have had no effect.

The man's body shudders, and he takes a rattling breath. He almost immediately starts to cough, opens his eyes, and with your help sits up. You have brought the mercenary back from the brink of death! Take +1 MYSTIC and -1 {FEARFUL}.

Turn to **31**.

286

"I didn't!" the wolfman snarls. "At least, that wasn't my intention."

"I thought you might be working together," says Moon Knight.

"Just because we were in the Legion of Monsters together? Talk about stereotyping! I had no idea N'Kantu was back in town, never mind why."

Take +1 {HAPPY HALLOWEEN}.

"There is evil afoot here," the Werewolf continues, "and we must sniff it out before its malign influence can spread any further."

Turn to **162**.

287

Taking the ray gun-like device in hand, you point the parabolic dish at the colossus and pull the trigger. A thrumming wall of sound bursts from the weapon, the concussive waves bombarding the stone giant.

The idol throws up its arms against the sonic attack. Even though you can see tiny cracks forming in its carved surface, the idol continues its relentless advance. You keep your finger pressed down on the trigger until the device's power cell is completely drained and the throbbing hum of the sonic disruptor is replaced by an unwelcome silence.

Take **+1 {FEARFUL}** and strike the **[Alien Device]** from your Inventory.

Turn to **149**.

288

You assume the same slack-jawed expression and lumbering gait as those who have already succumbed to the Curse of Akharis, imitating the way the Living Mummy is prone to walk, and stagger toward the TKTS steps, atop which stands the agent of Anubis. The Werewolf and Moon Knight do the same. At least you assume the vigilante assumes the same facial expression, but you can't tell because of his mask.

Make an acting test. Roll one die, and add your **MIND**, along with your **{GRANTED}**, if you have any. What is the result?

9 or more: take the ACHIEVEMENT: *Walk Like an Egyptian* and turn to **90**.

8 or less: turn to **299**.

289

At long last you enter the cavernous chamber that lies at the heart of the mountain. The whirling, kaleidoscopic light that fills the space sends flickering shadows dancing across its tapering walls, completely overwhelming the firelight emitted by burning braziers that stand at each corner of the room.

Considering everything you have experienced since N'Kantu burst out of the sarcophagus and battled Moon Knight at the Metropolitan Museum of Art, you shouldn't be surprised to see a muscular, human figure sat upon an ornate throne on the opposite side of the chamber, dressed in the manner of an Egyptian but with the head of a jackal upon his shoulders. Nonetheless you are still struck dumb and immobile by the sight – but then again, you are in the presence of a god. Take +2 {AWED}.

Anubis, god of the dead, turns his golden-eyed gaze upon you and you have to fight the desire to come to heel and kneel before him.

Sitting either side of Anubis's throne are two large jackals, their sleek coats as black as the interior of a cave at midnight.

Frozen to the spot as you are, you slowly take in the rest of the chamber, moving nothing but your eyes. Standing at Anubis's right hand is N'Kantu the Living Mummy, but standing to his left is someone whose presence here causes you to start in surprise, shaking you from your god-induced stupor.

It is Dr Uraeus, the recently appointed curator of the Metropolitan Museum of Art. His attire appears completely incongruous, given the company he is in. What's he doing here? Did N'Kantu kidnap him and bring him here under duress?

"Surprised to see me?" he asks. You nod dumbly in response to his question. "Just you wait. You haven't seen anything yet." You follow his gaze toward the apex of the chamber where the triangular walls converge.

Floating at the very center of the pyramid is the cursed canopic jar the Mummy stole from the exhibition. The hieroglyphs adorning its surface are pulsing with an infernal light. Swirling around the glowing jar is what you at first take to be mist until you begin to see shapes within the vaporous trails akin to screaming human faces.

It is just as you beheld in Times Square – human souls are being drawn into the jar, but it would appear that the pyramidal chamber itself is increasing its range and power somehow. It is only then that you notice the faintly glowing hieroglyphs covering the walls of the chamber, just like those on the jar. If the artifact is inscribed with spells taken from the Darkhold, then the chamber walls must be too, and they are amplifying the power of the soul-gathering ritual.

You realize then that Moon Knight is huddled on the ground beside you, physically incapacitated as well. But it is not the power of Anubis that has done this. An unpleasantly familiar voice sounds inside your head, so loud it is like a booming echo reverberating around the chamber. *Do it, Marc. Make the sacrifice! Kill the high priest!*

It is the voice of Khonshu – and you know that the high priest he is referring to is you!

If you have any {UNLOCKED}, {GRANTED} or {ECLIPSED}, which is highest?

If it is your {UNLOCKED}, turn to **271**.

If it is your {ECLIPSED}, turn to **183**.

If it is your {GRANTED}, turn to **146**.

If they are all identical in value, turn to **65**.

Doctor Strange told you that the [Orb of Belgaroth] can absorb dark magic, but as you hold it out before the monstrous serpent, it doesn't appear to have an effect. That is because Seth's powers of transformation are innate and divine, rather than being the result of casting some shapeshifting spell.

The creature's tail lashes out, hitting you in the chest and sending you flying. You hit the ground hard. The crystal ball flies from your grasp and collides with the wall behind you, smashing to smithereens upon impact.

Take -1 MIGHT and -1 {SNAKEBITE} and remove the [Orb of Belgaroth] from your Inventory.

There's no time to try anything else, as the enraged serpent strikes!

Turn to **192**.

291

It soon becomes apparent that Carson Knowles really shouldn't have tested Mr Knight, on tonight of all nights. The masked vigilante quickly takes him down with his weapon of choice.

Make a vigilante test. Roll one die.

If the number rolled is less than or equal to your {UNLOCKED}, turn to **185**.

If the number rolled is greater than your {UNLOCKED}, or you don't have any, turn to **136**.

292

Thanks to Moon Knight's skillful piloting, the drone soon catches up with his shadowy doppelganger. Your companion does not bother landing the craft before disembarking, but simply drops onto the roof where he has his counterpart cornered.

The drone touches down a moment later and you are glad to disembark yourself, just as the stranger says, "Ill met by moonlight. How are you, brother?"

Turn to **181**.

293

"Officer, we're on your side," Mr Knight says, modulating his voice to keep it at a low baritone. "I'm guessing you are dealing with a difficult situation and could use my help. I do, after all, possess some very specific skills that could make your problem go away. But the thing is, where I go, my associate goes too. So, if you would be so good as to lower your gun and step out of our way…"

As if in a trance, the cop does just that. Take +1 {ECLIPSED}.

Turn to **34**.

The two of you follow the tunnel, which leads you deeper into the baking bedrock of the mountain. The walls are of the same dressed stone you have seen everywhere else, covered with a layer of plaster, on top of which have been painted scenes of the gods in the most vibrant colors. The passageway is lit by flickering torches, which create the illusion that the painted figures are moving.

Eventually the passageway turns left, and you find the dressed stone gives way to rough-hewn walls. Not much further on, the path you are following comes to an end at a great void in the ground. It appears to be a natural chimney that runs up and down through the mountain. You do not dare to think what might lie at the bottom in its black depths, but you can just make out a ledge on the far side with a passageway leading away from it.

"I am confident I could glide across the gap using my cape alone," Moon Knight says, "but Khonshu says we both need to be present to stop Anubis and bring about a successful conclusion to our quest."

"A case of two heads are better than one?" you say.

"Unless you're the Bi-Beast. Come on, you're an expert in ancient Egyptian tombs. How do you think we should negotiate this obstacle?"

You think for a minute. "We could swing across?"

"Genius. Now, why didn't I think of that?"

While you might have suggested it, how do you really

feel about swinging across the void with Moon Knight?

If you are prepared to give it a go, turn to **283**.

If you would prefer to retrace your steps and take the other route, turn to **76**.

295

You open the leatherbound tome, its spine cracking as you do so. It falls open at a page bearing a spell entitled "How to Raise a Man from the Dead." As you scan the page, the esoteric script that covers the faded vellum sears itself onto your eyeballs and, as if at the behest of the book, you feel compelled to recite the words out loud.

You can feel the power of the [Black Grimoire] burning through you. Take +1 {DARK POWER}.

Turn to **31**.

296

"Good idea," your companion says, setting off down the museum steps, making for the nearest entrance to the park. You must jog to keep up, but even though you are soon out of breath, you get the impression Moon Knight is taking it easy for your sake.

You still can't get your head around the fact that you heard Khonshu speak and are now pursuing a millennia old Mummy through Central Park.

Suddenly the stillness of the park is disturbed by the hooting of primates and the snarling of predators. The noise is coming from the Central Park Zoo.

"Do you think that has something to do with our quarry?" Moon Knight asks.

You find yourself taken aback. Why does a super hero like Moon Knight care what you think?

"Come on, tell me your thoughts," he challenges you. "Khonshu says that your presence is vital, so here's an opportunity for you to prove yourself.

So, what do you think the pair of you should do?

To stick to the route you are following through the park, turn to **272**.

To change direction and head toward the zoo, turn to **242**.

"Time is pressing, and you must be on your way. Follow me."

Doctor Strange promptly levitates, thanks to the magical cloak he wears, and leads you on a winding route through the house, until at last you enter the very definition of a wizard's inner sanctum.

The room is dominated by a distinctive circular window, the frame of which you are convinced forms what must be some arcane rune. Outside, against the ambient glow of the light pollution that hangs over Manhattan Island, you fancy you glimpse figures swinging, flying, and elongating across the sky. Other heroes have joined the fight to save the city from the zombies.

"It is the Anomaly Rue," Strange says, seeing you staring at the window, "the Seal of the Vishanti. It helps protect the Sanctum Sanctorum from magical attacks – and it will help me now in opening a portal to send you after N'Kantu."

The sorcerer approaches an old-fashioned globe that stands in one corner of the room. As he waves his hands over it, muttering something under his breath, you see the Anomaly Rue rune appear in purple, hovering over the eastern seaboard of North America, pinpointing the location of the Sanctum Sanctorum.

Strange continues to make arcane gestures, whilst still muttering to himself, and a second symbol appears over

North Africa. This symbol looks like an Ankh and glows yellow.

"There we have it!" the wizard announces triumphantly. "As I thought, your quarry has taken his prize to Egypt."

"Of course," Moon Knight throws in.

Doctor Strange begins to form swirling patterns with his arms and a pinwheel of orange sparks bursts into being. As he continues with the spiraling gesture, the circle widens, opening a window that looks out onto another world. While the room you are in is shrouded in gloom, lit only by glowing lanterns and flickering candlelight, through the hole in the air you can see the brilliant blue of sky, dazzling daylight, and a sandy desert.

Your eyes widen in wonder as you catch sight of the endless sands, and an as yet unanswered question surfaces within your mind once more.

"Doctor Strange," you begin, "do you know why Khonshu calls me 'high priest'?"

As the Sorcerer Supreme opens his mouth, as if to answer, an explosion shakes the Sanctum Sanctorum to its very foundations.

"The enemy are at the gates!" Moon Knight says.

"Hurry!" the Sorcerer Supreme snaps. "Step through the portal! I am needed elsewhere."

The portal is wide enough for you a pass through now. Without a moment's hesitation, Moon Knight leaps through it. Taking a moment to steady yourself, not daring to consider the impossibility of what you are doing, you follow…

Make a teleportation test. Roll two dice, add your **MIND**, and deduct any {**DARK POWER**} you may have. What's the result?

Total of 12 or more: turn to **27**.

11 or less: turn to **45**.

298

"Our priority has to be catching up with the Living Mummy," Moon Knight says, "but should we go high or stay low?"

How will you reply?

"Go high." Turn to **42**.

"Stay low." Turn to **106**.

299

Time is running out, comes the voice of the moon god, hissing like the grains emptying from the bulb of a sand timer.

Those who have already been turned into mindless zombies howl, as if with one voice, and turn on you.

If you have a {HUNTED} of 3, turn to **152**.

If you have a {HUNTED} of 1 or 2, turn to **140**.

If you have not acquired the {HUNTED} quality, turn to **168**.

300

A swirl of amber sparks suddenly fizzes into existence a few feet above the ground close to where you are standing. It expands with every spiraling rotation until you can make out another gloomy room on the other side. But rather than being another subterranean, brazier-lit chamber, this one is filled with bookshelves and magical paraphernalia. And there, amidst it all, you can see the one who has opened the portal – Doctor Stephen Strange.

"Hurry, you fools!" he snaps, the infernal Darkhold hieroglyphs flaring, as if in response to his magical meddling. "You don't have much time!" As if to emphasize his point, sand starts to pour from a crack that has opened at the apex of the pyramidal space.

The three of you step through without a second thought, and the portal snaps shut.

ACHIEVEMENT: *Fast Travel.*

"Thank you, truly," says Moon Knight, moving to look out of the round window that dominates the wizard's sanctuary. You and Frenchie join him there.

It is still night on this side of the globe but the street outside the Sanctum Sanctorum no longer rings with the howls of the undead or the sounds of battle. You can see people milling about in confusion, zombies no more.

"Not to put too fine a point on it, Marc Spector," Doctor Strange says, addressing Moon Knight, "but you have saved the world."

"I have done no more than my duty as Khonshu's avatar and protector of those who travel by night," Moon Knight replies.

The Fist of Khonshu might be in a humble mood, but you take a moment to consider that you helped save the world, too. And there aren't many Egyptologists who can say that.

ACHIEVEMENT: *All in a Day's Work*.

Final score: 4 stars.

The End.

ACHIEVEMENTS CHECKLIST

As you find these ACHIEVEMENTS in play, check them off the list!

- ☐ *A Close Call*
- ☐ *All in a Day's Work*
- ☐ *Awkward Questions*
- ☐ *Big Bang*
- ☐ *City of the Dead*
- ☐ *Code Red*
- ☐ *Codebreaker*
- ☐ *Could Do Better*
- ☐ *Dead and Buried*
- ☐ *Discretion is the Better Part of Valor*
- ☐ *Divine Inspiration*
- ☐ *Fast Travel*
- ☐ *Fetch!*
- ☐ *For Luck*
- ☐ *French Kissing*
- ☐ *Genius Level Intellect*
- ☐ *Geography Lesson*
- ☐ *Going Underground*
- ☐ *Gone to the Dogs*
- ☐ *I Think We Took a Wrong Turn*
- ☐ *Late Night Double Feature*
- ☐ *Life Saver*

- ☐ *Mummy's Boy*
- ☐ *Necessity is the Mother of Invention*
- ☐ *Night of the Hunter*
- ☐ *Night of the Living Dead*
- ☐ *Now That's Magic!*
- ☐ *Off the Leash*
- ☐ *Okey-dokey, Dr Jones*
- ☐ *Overkill*
- ☐ *Resurrection*
- ☐ *Russian Roulette*
- ☐ *Scholar*
- ☐ *Secret One*
- ☐ *Secret Two*
- ☐ *Secret Three*
- ☐ *Secret Four*
- ☐ *Son et Lumiere*
- ☐ *Super Hero Sidekick*
- ☐ *Take Flight*
- ☐ *The Dog Whisperer*
- ☐ *The Ultimate Sacrifice*
- ☐ *Tomb Raider*
- ☐ *Trophy Hunter*
- ☐ *Walk Like an Egyptian*
- ☐ *Wall of Sound*

SUPER-ACHIEVEMENTS CHECKLIST

☐ Finish with a combined **MIGHT + MIND + MYSTIC** of 20 or more: *Mighty*.

☐ Finish with at least two stars and a combined **MIGHT + MIND + MYSTIC** of 5 or less: *Cutting it Close*.

☐ Finish with 1 or 0 stars: *Total Wipeout*.

☐ Finish with {**UNLOCKED**} of 10 or more: *Psycho*.

☐ Finish with {**GRANTED**} of 5 or more: *Erudite*.

☐ Finish with {**ECLIPSED**} of 5 or more: *Moonstruck*.

☐ Finish with {**HAPPY HALLOWEEN**} of 3: *Legion of Monsters*.

☐ Finish with {**WHO LET THE DOGS OUT?**} of 3: *Release the Hounds*.

☐ Finish with {**ABRACADABRA**} of 5: *The Sorcerer's Apprentice*.

☐ Finish with {**FEARFUL**} of 5 or more: *Scaredy Cat*.

☐ Finish with {**SNAKEBITE**} of 5 of more: *Defanged*.

☐ Finish without cheating even once: *Angelic Avenger*.

☐ Battle N'Kantu the Living Mummy, Werewolf, and Manphibian: *Monster Mash*.

☐ Use both the [**Tactical Grenade**] and [**Sticks of Dynamite**] in one playthrough: *Demolition Man*.

☐ Finish with a **[Khopesh]**, an **[Ankh]**, and the **[Eye of Horus]**: *It Belongs in a Museum!*

☐ Finish with **[Whip]**, **[Tactical Grenade]**, **[Vial of Serum]**, **[Crossbow]**, and **[Alien Device]**: *Trophy Cabinet.*

☐ Discover all 13 items across various playthroughs: *Kleptomaniac.*

☐ Discover all 4 starred endings: *Determined.*

☐ Discover all 11 deaths: *Accident Prone.*

☐ Discover all 4 Secret achievements: *No Stone Unturned.*

☐ Collect all 20 super-achievements above this one: *Rigorous.*

☐ Collect all 46 in-text achievements: *Relentless.*

☐ And if you collect both *Rigorous* and *Relentless,* award yourself *Champion of Champions.*

ACKNOWLEDGMENTS

I've had a blast playing with Moon Knight in the Marvel sandbox. I have loved Marvel comics since I was a child, which is when my obsession with ancient Egyptian myth also began, so to be able to work on a project that married the two has been a dream come true.

I would like to thank Aconyte's publisher, Marc Gascoigne, for the initial invitation, and Gwendolyn Nix for her expert editorial support throughout. And lastly, a huge thank you must go to Victor Cheng, as ever, for his invaluable, not to mention meticulous, playtesting.

ABOUT THE AUTHOR

JONATHAN GREEN is an award-winning writer of speculative fiction with more than eighty books to his name. He has written everything from *Fighting Fantasy* gamebooks to *Doctor Who* novels, by way of *Sonic the Hedgehog*, *Star Wars: The Clone Wars*, *Teenage Mutant Ninja Turtles*, and *Judge Dredd*. He is the creator of the *Pax Britannia* steampunk series for Abaddon Books, and the author of the critically acclaimed, *YOU ARE THE HERO – A History of Fighting Fantasy Gamebooks*. He is currently writing his own ACE Gamebooks, which reimagine literary classics as interactive adventures.

To find out more about his current projects visit *JonathanGreenAuthor.com*, or follow him on Twitter *@jonathangreen* and on Instagram *@jongreen71*.

HEROES NEED YOUR HELP

BE THE SIDEKICK YOU WERE BORN TO BE & CHOOSE THE WAY OF THE HERO!

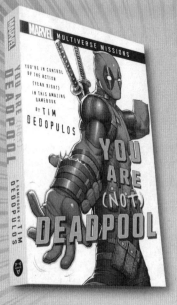

Deadpool forces you to defeat predictability (and sure, okay, some bad crime lords along the way) through mini-games and puzzles in this new adventure gamebook!

Embark on an adventure with She-Hulk to uncover a sinister plot from destroying the world where your choices – and chance – drive the story!

EPIC SUPER POWERS
AMAZING AVENTURES

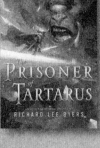